Along These Highways

Camino del Sol

A Latina and Latino Literary Series

Along These Highways

stories by
Rene S. Perez II

THE UNIVERSITY OF
ARIZONA PRESS

TUCSON

THE UNIVERSITY OF ARIZONA PRESS

www.uapress.arizona.edu

Library of Congress Cataloging-in-Publication Data

Perez, Rene S., 1984–

Along these highways : stories / by Rene S. Perez II.

  p. cm. — (Camino del sol: a Latina and Latino literary series)

ISBN 978-0-8165-3010-6 (pbk. : acid-free paper)

I. Title.

PS3616.E74346A79 2012

813'.6—dc23

                    2011030693

Publication of this book is made possible in part by the proceeds of a permanent endowment created with the assistance of a Challenge Grant from the National Endowment for the Humanities,
a federal agency.

♻

Manufactured in the United States of America on acid-free, archival-quality paper containing a
minimum of 30% post-consumer waste and processed chlorine free.

17   16   15   14   13   12   6   5   4   3   2   1

For Ulyana—
I've got the writing thing down;
keep inspiring me to be.

Contents

Along These Highways

One Last Drive North

"This place doesn't have a thirteenth floor," Alfredo says out loud, not noticing the woman standing next to him in the elevator. She looks at him and gives him a shrug that tells him she doesn't much care to share in his observations. Alfredo reads her body language for what it is and is content standing at his corner of the elevator with his mouth shut. He is genuinely surprised, however, that in all his trips to this hospital, he has never noticed that it does not have a thirteenth floor. She gets off the elevator at the eleventh floor, a floor Alfredo knows to be an intensive care floor, and he rides up to his destination alone. He gets off the elevator on the top floor, the one marked "22," the one he now knows to be the twenty-first. Alfredo doesn't come to this hospital very much, though there was a time when he did.

Up until fifteen years ago, Alfredo could smoke in the solarium on the top floor of the hospital. Nowadays, smoking isn't allowed within twenty-five feet of any of its entrances. Alfredo doesn't mind the new rules like he used to. When they first went into effect, he made more frequent trips to the hospital and was still a smoker. He no longer smokes, but not because it has become socially unacceptable. He no longer gets the same pleasure that he used to from smoking. He used to love the nicotine buzz that was ever so slight compared to any other drug, and so fleeting that he'd need to smoke a chain of cigarettes just to constantly feel that minor, straight-headed, clear-eyed high. Now that he's older, Alfredo realizes that he was putting up with the headaches and bad lungs to hold on to a pleasure that morphed into a routine, a necessity, and that died as a plaguing habit.

The view from the floor labeled "22" at the hospital has changed drastically in the decades since Alfredo first came to Dallas. Now all he sees are billboards and skyscrapers and smog. He has never been able to understand how this place, one that has always been so huge, has continued to grow nonstop. There are always construction crews working on buildings,

1

extending roadways, making things new—newer. At home, everything seems to stay the same.

Greenton, Texas, has remained close to exactly the same small town Alfredo was born in, with three gas stations, two general stores, and the Dairy Queen across the street from the courthouse. The only additions that have been made to Greenton in the last sixty-seven years are a supermarket and a liquor store. The supermarket's groceries are overpriced, inflated because if anyone in Greenton wants to buy groceries in bulk anywhere else, they have to travel thirty-five miles to Falfurrias, where prices are also inflated, though slightly less so than in Greenton.

When the liquor store opened twenty-one years ago, the people of Greenton were split on whether it was good or evil. The liquor store's prices are also high, but not only for convenience. It was decided, at a Greenton Town Hall meeting, that there would be a 4 percent local tax, on top of the state sales tax, to raise money for the Greenton school system, and to appease the town's Guadalupanas and Knights of Columbus, who seemed to think the rows of bottles in a corner store in downtown Greenton meant the coming of the apocalypse.

Both of these businesses do well, despite the fact that their customers end up paying too much for too little, because there is no competition for what they are pushing.

Alfredo has always been impressed by the Dallas skyline, but the sight has also always saddened him with what its constant state of progress implies about Greenton. Alfredo stands looking out for only a few minutes. Then he goes back into the elevator and presses the "B" button. It's time for him to work.

People get on the elevator at the fifteenth, seventh, and fourth floors, but they all get off in the lobby. Alfredo usually rides to the basement alone. He walks into the morgue of the hospital and declares his business.

"I'm here from the Greenton Funeral home, to pick up the body of Efrain Ochoa," he tells the morgue supervisor.

Alfredo goes with her to pick up the body from a refrigerated storage area and is given a clipboard with papers to sign to release the cargo he has come to transport.

"You must be new here," he says as he signs his papers. "I've never seen you."

She lights up at Alfredo talking to her and smiles as she zips up Efrain Ochoa's body bag. The morgue attendants always brighten whenever Alfredo talks to them. He came to the conclusion, years ago, that a certain social awkwardness is an occupational hazard in dealing with so many more dead people than living ones. At least in owning a funeral home, more than half of the people he deals with are alive. Apart from the countless corpses, this poor girl mainly deals only with people like Alfredo and a few other morgue attendants.

"I started last month. It's an easy job. It's just so cold," she says sheepishly, looking over the signed papers. "It seems like you come here often; I guess that means we'll be seeing each other a lot."

She seems genuine in her interest, and so Alfredo thinks on this for a second before answering. With a polite smile, he lies. "Sure."

The supervisor, whose name he learns is Magdalene, hands Alfredo a cup of coffee before he takes the body to the loading dock by way of the freight elevator. As he waits for the slow machine to carry him up the single floor separating the back of the morgue and the loading dock, Alfredo is tempted to unzip the body bag and take a look at what the years away from Greenton have done to his old friend Efrain Ochoa, the man everyone in Greenton knew as Frankie. If the elevator ride were a few minutes longer, Alfredo just might succumb to the curious temptation that makes him want so badly to disregard protocol and propriety.

When the massive doors open to the loading dock, Ramon is there waiting for Alfredo. He is leaning on the side of the hearse and still has cheese dust on his fingers from the potato chips he had been eating.

"What took you so long?" he asks.

Alfredo looks at his son, at his disheveled hair and untucked shirt, and can think of nothing to tell him.

"Just get in the car." That is all he can say.

The drive home is fairly quiet. Ramon is drinking his soda and eating the rest of his potato chips as Alfredo drives. Alfredo frequently comments to Ramon about the drive, trying to remind him of the way to get home.

"Remember to get off on 16. You have to get on 16 south or you'll end up in Laredo," Alfredo says, growing impatient at the sight of his son's know-it-all smile. "Are you listening to me? This is important. I won't always be here to give you directions, goddamn it!"

At this point, Alfredo realizes he is yelling. He calms down and looks over to see Ramon still smiling.

"I know the way to the cities like the back of my hand. How many times have we made this drive since I was a kid? From the home it's Main to 16 to 37 to 35. I know how to get to these hospitals like it's nothing. You worry too much," Ramon says.

Alfredo is annoyed by how relaxed Ramon is during such a serious conversation, but he knows that his son is right.

The rest of the trip home is silent, until they are forty-five miles outside of Greenton.

The first drop of rain falls fat and hard on the top driver's-side corner of the windshield. Alfredo sees it there, shaking and being pushed by the oncoming wind to the top of the windshield, then out of sight. The drop was there less than half a minute, and Alfredo hopes that Ramon did not notice it. When the next three raindrops fall, fatter and harder, from the hot, late-afternoon sky onto the windshield, Alfredo knows that Ramon has noticed them, and he hopes beyond reason that more do not follow.

Alfredo drives on, his thumbnails clawing furrows into the steering wheel, and his eyes straining to focus. When the rain starts falling consistently, the silence that was comfortable enough for the first two hundred miles of the trip becomes aggravating and taunts Alfredo with the possibility of his son speaking up. Alfredo tries his best to not look at Ramon, but he can feel the car become smaller as he sees, peripherally, Ramon sit up in his seat. With his soda and his potato chips finished, Ramon has never seemed more grown up than he is right now, concerned that he might have to confront his stubborn father.

"You all right, Dad?" Ramon asks. The question is a badly disguised front for what Alfredo knows his son is saying.

"Yeah," Alfredo says. "It's not that dark. It's not even raining that hard."

And, with that, Mother Nature decides to contradict Alfredo. Just as he comments on the weather, a clap of thunder provides an exclamation mark for his sentence. Storm clouds form in the minutes-ago-clear sky; they were nowhere to be seen on the horizon up to this point. The rain, which was initially just annoying in its relentlessness, begins its assault on the highway and, more so, on Alfredo. Just a few short minutes after Alfredo spoke, the light of day that was helping the visibility on the road disappears. Clouds and rain collude to blind him, to end his trip.

"I think you're going to have to pull over. It's really dark out," Ramon says calmly, seeming to know very well how his father will take such an encroachment.

Alfredo's grip on the steering wheel becomes even tighter. He has not felt this angry and helpless since he was first told, by his doctor, that he would not be able to drive at night or in the dark. Ramon, no longer tense and with a calmness and patience that reminds Alfredo of his late wife, Ramon's mother, says again, "Dad, you have to pull over and let me drive."

"I can see, goddamn it. Even if I was blind, I could make this drive. I've done it so many times," Alfredo says, surprised at his voice crescendoing to a shout. "Don't tell me what to do."

Ramon is still calm. "I know you can get us there, Dad, it's just that the doctor said . . ." His voice trails off, and then he concedes. "Fine, take us home."

He is sure he can make it home, no matter how dark it is outside. He feels fine, even though streetlights and the headlights of the cars around him blur together in his eyes, blinding streaks of white and gold standing out in the black world around them. Regardless of how sure he is of himself, he knows what he has to do. He pulls the hearse onto the highway shoulder and waits for Ramon to get out of the car so he can scoot over to the passenger's seat.

"About how many times have you gone to get bodies from the big cities, Dad?" Ramon asks, after pulling back onto the highway.

"Hundreds of times," Alfredo says calmly, as though he had not just shouted at his son in a childish fit of anger. "I even drove into Louisiana once to get a body. It seems like even when people make it out of Greenton, they still want to be buried there."

Ramon laughs at this.

"Where's the farthest you've gotten a body from?" he asks next.

Alfredo doesn't even have to think about this. "Vietnam. I picked up three bodies in San Antonio that were flown in from Vietnam."

"Really? There were three people from Greenton who fought in Vietnam?"

Alfredo smiles. "No, there were five. Jaime Gruy and Jose Fernandez also went."

This surprises Ramon. "'El Feo' Fernandez?" he asks.

"The same. Why do you think he became a drunk? He saw too much over there."

They are quiet for a while. "Goddamn," Ramon says to himself.

"Hey, watch your mouth," Alfredo says, pointing at the body in back. "Frankie Ochoa was a holy roller. We were good friends when we were kids. But when his mom died, he started getting into a lot of trouble. He was a real thug in high school. He even threw a few beatings my way, but then he got into a bad car accident, and after that, his left leg was longer than his right, and he'd never stop talking about God and Jesus. He moved to the city to preach. He sure was wild when we were kids, though." After saying this, Alfredo looks in the rearview mirror at the bag that holds Frankie's earthly remains.

5

"Oh yeah, isn't he Omar Ochoa's uncle?" Ramon asks.

"Yes, this is him," Alfredo answers. No matter how far a person goes in the world, Alfredo thinks, if they are from Greenton, there will always be a town of people who will know their name for generations, whether or not they ever look back.

The conversation shortens the last forty-five minutes of the trip, and in what seems to Alfredo like no time at all, they are home. The men get out of the hearse and take the stretcher from the back, wheeling it inside, taking Efrain Ochoa out of his body bag and placing him onto the examination table in the back of the funeral home, which doubles as Alfredo's home.

"I'm going, Dad. I'll be here tomorrow morning to help you with Mr. Ochoa here," Ramon says.

"Okay, tell Gina I said hi." Alfredo doesn't look at his son as he says this. His eyes are fixed on the grey face of his old friend.

Ramon waves goodbye to his father, who doesn't notice, and leaves for home, a house he and his wife bought three years ago, just two blocks from his father. Alfredo stands for a while in the back room of the funeral parlor. He looks down at the corpse that was Frankie Ochoa. He thinks of when they were in middle school, how they would play together in gym and talk together in lunch. Alfredo can't remember, in detail, any of the games they played, nor can he remember what either of them had to say in their adolescent conversations. Has it really been that long since they were friends? Alfredo can remember the triumphant, somewhat apologetic look on Frankie's face when he said he was leaving Greenton, just after graduation. Alfredo remembers feeling envious, and not much else, of the fact that Frankie was leaving. They had grown apart in Frankie's delinquent days, and by the time he found God, they were already done as friends.

This all happened years ago. Alfredo had not thought of Frankie Ochoa much, if at all, in that time. When he heard that it was Frankie Ochoa whom he would be picking up today, on his last trip north, to Dallas, he was happy.

After a few minutes of thinking, Alfredo goes outside and sits down in the chair on his front porch, smelling the rain in the air and staring out to watch the dusky evening turn to night. In those moments when his house is extra silent or cold, Alfredo thinks back to the times when he would go out to the porch and have a smoke. Now, in the still, idle minutes when Alfredo is sitting to pass time, even the porch is a lonely place.

In forty-five years, Alfredo has come to prepare for burial the bodies of every single person who has died in Greenton, or whose wish it was to be buried there, with the exception of only two people. He couldn't bring himself to work on his wife after the car crash. He was too shocked when it happened, less than ten years ago. Someone had to be called in from Bruni to prepare his wife's body for her funeral.

While he didn't work on his daughter either, he did drive up to Austin in the hearse to pick up her body from the cancer ward of St. David's Hospital. On that day, twenty years ago, Alfredo made the drive alone and cried the whole way home as he agonized over the life that his beautiful daughter, who was lying peacefully a mere three feet away from him, could have had.

He will still work on the bodies of people who want to be buried in Greenton. His old school friends and teachers, the local sheriffs and drunks, the old people he remembers from their better days, and the unfortunate children who will never get to grow up—Alfredo will still work on all of them. Efrain Ochoa, however, has the distinction of being the last body that Alfredo will ever drive up north to pick up.

He can still ride with his son if he so chooses, but Alfredo's never really been able to ride along on a long drive, he gets too bored. When the doctor told Alfredo, a month ago, that he has bad night vision and that he probably shouldn't drive at all, but definitely never at night, he made a declaration that day, which was not objected to by either Ramon or the doctor, that he would make one last drive up north. It saddens Alfredo that he won't take any more of his trips out of Greenton, the trips that always offered him a brief escape from a life that has always suited him, but one that has also bored him from time to time. He is glad, however, that Ramon will be able to do it instead.

Despite how hard he rides Ramon, he's proud of him. He's sure of him. There was a time when Alfredo thought that Ramon would never be able to recover from the death of his mother, but he made it out of the darkness, as he had when his sister died; he even found a wife who would move to Greenton with him.

It took him six years away at college, but Ramon got his degree in mortuary sciences. For a while, Alfredo thought Ramon would never come home, and that he would have to run the funeral home by himself, but Ramon made it. Alfredo is glad, because he knows that when he dies, the home, and the people of Greenton, will be in good hands. He is also glad because he knows that while he is alive he won't have to be alone.

After sitting on the porch for what seems a long time, Alfredo makes himself a sandwich and watches television. But after a few hours of watching mostly commercials, he still isn't tired. He cleans up, goes to the room in the back of the house, and starts working on Frankie Ochoa.

Once Alfredo puts on his apron and a pair of gloves, he no longer thinks of Frankie as an old friend. He is now a body to be prepared like any other body Alfredo has ever worked on. Alfredo begins by washing the body with an olfactant/germicide–insecticide solution. After the body is washed, he uses cotton to swab the solution in Frankie's mouth, nose, and eyes. Then, slowly and carefully, perhaps with more care than usual, Alfredo massages rigor mortis out of Frankie's body. He then rubs a cream on Frankie's cold, rubbery face, deep into the tissue, to soften and loosen its muscles, and smoothes out the indentions that breathing tubes left there. Despite how long it has been since Alfredo last saw Frankie, he does not have to refer to a picture when setting his face. He places the eye caps and mouth former on Frankie, and then sutures his mouth shut from the inside. Alfredo then drains the blood out of Frankie's body and fills it with a mixture of formaldehyde and water. The embalming of Frankie Ochoa is complete when Alfredo uses a trocar to aspirate the gas and fluids from his torso, filling it with a stronger concentration of formaldehyde, and, finally, when Alfredo sews up the hole caused by the trocar. Alfredo then washes the body again and dries it off carefully.

Once this is done, Alfredo begins working on Frankie's makeup. It is close to four o'clock in the morning when Alfredo finishes. He is finally tired. He thinks of the day to come and knows it will just be another boring one in Greenton. It is then that Alfredo is saddest that he has made his last drive up to the big cities in Texas, or anywhere else. He thinks for a minute and then turns off the lights in the back room. As he stands in the door-way, the light from the hall shines in on the body of Efrain Ochoa, the man Alfredo knew by a different name, in a different life. Seeing Frankie there, a work of art created of memory and of compassion and of care, Alfredo is no longer sad. A weight is lifted from his shoulders, and he doesn't think when the words come to his mouth—

"God bless you, Frankie. God bless you."

Curses by Numbers

Benny stood for a second in the doorway, taking in the sights, sounds, and smells of Flojo's before walking in. He hadn't been in the bar in six and a half years, and it felt like coming home. Nothing had changed. Vicente and Liz hadn't gotten rid of the big-screen TV in the back of the bar, which hadn't worked since the last time the Cowboys won the Super Bowl; the felt was still torn on the pool table directly in front of the bar, and the other one was still propped up by a stack of magazines to even out the lean that sent all shots to one corner; the songs on the jukebox hadn't been updated; it seemed that the ice in the trough in the men's room hadn't melted and been replaced—the piss-caked sticky on the floor certainly hadn't been cleaned; and Benny felt even more at home knowing that he'd contributed to the stickiness that held to the bottom of his shoes, pleading for him not to leave again.

After he took the tour (walked around the place once, then took a leak), Benny sat at the bar and asked Liz for a Bud. He expected her to acknowledge his return after so long. When she didn't, he realized it was because her attention was devoted to a man slouched over on his stool at the end of the bar. Benny had initially ignored the man, letting him wallow in his drunk alone. When he looked closer, he recognized the man's ball cap, looked below its bill, and saw the fatter, now wrinkled face, reddened from drink, of a man he'd called a friend in days gone by.

"Gumby!" Benny shouted, his decision to return having been validated by the sight of the drunken man. He scooted over the four stools that separated them and slapped his friend on the back. In a concentrated rush of anger that Benny wouldn't have expected from a man so far gone into his night, Gumby bucked his head up and swung the bottle in his hand, neck first, at Benny.

Aside from being splashed by what was left in Gumby's bottle, Benny wasn't hurt. He was grateful that he hadn't had his first for the night, much less his seventh, eighth, or ninth, because if he hadn't reacted so quickly, Gumby would have cut a new mouth in the side of his face.

Gumby fell off his stool with the force of his swing. Benny grabbed his arms below the shoulders, and the two of them fell slowly and awkwardly to the floor. Arms wrapped around his friend, Benny tried to calm him down.

"Gumby, it's me. Benny." He leveled his eyes with Gumby's when they stood up. Gumby's eyes lit in recognition. He situated himself on his barstool.

"Bring us two Buds," he yelled at Liz, who had gone to the kitchen. "Benny, man, I haven't seen you in years."

"Gumby, we see each other in church every Sunday."

"I know that, pendejo. But in here, at Flojo's." Gumby smiled, gave Benny a pat on the back, and slapped hard on the bar. "Liz, beers!"

Liz came back to the bar carrying two cases of beer. She put them down and handed Benny a cold longneck. "It's great to see you. I know it's been a while since you've been in, but let me tell you, he's not driving home. If you don't take him, I'll have to call his mom to get him."

"Don't worry. I'll get him home," Benny said and took a drink of his beer.

"So how've you been, Ben?" she asked with her back to him, putting beers from the case into the cooler behind the bar.

"Good, you know. I've just been working and all that." Benny could hear the conversation he was about to have play out in his head and made the decision to lie his way past the embarrassing and painful parts.

"Where's Yoli?" Liz asked, like Benny knew she would. "At home with your boy?"

Benny nodded in agreement. "And Vicente?" he asked, changing the focus without changing the subject. As if his delicateness could change the truth of what he was lying about.

"His brother in Chicago is real sick," she said. "He went to help out. So what's Yoli up to these days?" she asked, and Benny was happy when Gumby interrupted. He didn't have it in him to make up a happy life.

"Hey, is this a high school reunion or a bar? Will any booze be served at this pachanga, or should I have snuck in a bottle of the hard stuff to put in the punch?" Gumby said, trying for playful but coming off like an ass. Liz rolled her eyes, popped the top off a beer, and handed it to him. He took it with a bow as she walked away, seemingly to keep from slugging him.

"To the return of Benny Guajardo." Gumby raised his drink and looked around the bar as if there weren't only three people in the place.

"May it signal a change in the alignment of the moon, sun, stars, or whatever's fucked my luck so bad." He offered his bottle over, and Benny tapped the top of his bottle to his friend's.

"How long have you been here?" Benny asked.

"All day."

"So, since five?"

"No, since they opened up. I didn't go in to work today." He got up, walked to the jukebox, and came back to the bar. "You got any quarters?" he asked Benny.

"Sorry. So why'd you skip work? Blue Monday?"

"It didn't feel safe, working those machines, all those pipes constantly moving around." He charades-mimed pipes overhead moving left to right and right to left. "You know, I've seen a guy lose his two big fingers when two pipes hit. The kid was too cocky to wear the gloves. And I've seen someone with the gloves on get their bones crushed—all four fingers were just dangling by the skin that had been protected by the leather. And with my luck being the way it is, I just knew I'd die if I went in." He looked at the big fingers on his left hand and took a drink of his beer.

Benny smiled. Gumby had always been a little funny. "What are you talking about? What's wrong with your luck?"

"I don't even want to talk about it."

"No, I want to hear why you skipped work today." Benny couldn't help but laugh as he took a drink of his beer.

Gumby reached into his pockets and pulled out six little sheets of paper. He tried to straighten them out, but they were falling onto the bar and down to the ground. "These, Benny. These." He pushed them into Benny's face and dropped them on the bar in front of him.

"What, lottery tickets? This is what has you worried about your luck? No one wins the lottery." He was laughing hard now. It was conversations like this that he'd missed, that he knew would be waiting for him at Flojo's. Gumby and his theories, Benny could tell himself that's why he came back.

"No, goddamn it! You don't get it. You won't get it." Gumby shook his head and got up to leave.

"Don't go, buddy. Don't go. I'm sorry. Explain it to me, please." Benny was trying to suppress his laughter. He didn't want to hurt an old friend. "I'm sorry. Believe me, my luck's been bad too."

"It all started on Thursday. My mom wanted me to pick up some chorizo and eggs from Circle C after work. When I get there, I see a ten-dollar bill on the ground. And then—"

"Well, that's good luck. Right?" Gumby shot Benny a look. "Sorry. Keep going."

"I pick it up and I decide—what the hell? It's not my money anyway. I might as well let it ride. You know?" Gumby nodded his head, as if cuing to Benny that now he could interject.

"The lottery tickets," Benny offered.

"Exactly. So I go in, buy the chorizo and eggs for my mom, and I get a few tickets. I got the Texas Two Step—" he pointed one out—"because the drawing was that Thursday. I got the Mega Millions because the drawing was on Friday." He pointed out another. "And I got the regular lotto ticket for the Saturday drawing. Simple as that. I got the tickets and I'm still up seven dollars."

"Okay," Benny said.

"I was here during the drawings on Thursday and Friday. I didn't get to see if my numbers won. So I went to the store on Saturday and had the cashier scan the Texas Two Step and Mega Millions. I lost." Gumby paused, shook his head, and took a drink from his beer.

"So that's your bad luck?" Benny asked.

"No. When I was at the store, I remembered the seven dollars and thought that even if they weren't the exact same dollars, I still had seven to play with and not lose anything. So I bought a Pick 5 and a couple of Pick 3s, because they'd all be drawn with the Lotto ticket that night.

"I was here again that night. I didn't see the drawing. But on Sunday, when I woke up, I got my father's paper to check the numbers."

"And you lost?" Benny offered. He was tired, bored, and ready to go home.

"Of course I lost. Would I be here if I'd won?"

Benny rolled his eyes and nodded his head, but Gumby kept on.

"I lost every drawing. Both Pick 3s, the Pick 5, and the Pick 6."

"That's not bad luck, Gumby, that's just probability. I think it's time for us to head home." Benny motioned to Liz for two more and the tab.

"This is where the bad luck comes in, why I can't go to work. Seeing the numbers all laid out on the paper, I noticed something. You see, they also had the results from the Texas Two Step and the Mega Millions from earlier that week printed out. I still had the losing tickets in my pocket from the day before. When I laid them all out"—Gumby took the tickets from Benny and laid them out in two rows of three—"I saw that the five numbers I'd picked for the Texas Two Step were the winning numbers for the Pick 5." Gumby pointed the tickets out to Benny. "And the six numbers I'd picked for the regular Lotto, they were the numbers that won for the Mega Millions. See," he pointed out, "they're the five numbers and the bonus ball. And to make it even weirder, the numbers I got for the two Pick 3s were the winning numbers for the regular Lotto. That's 78,547,000 dollars I would've won."

"Bullshit," Benny said. "That's impossible. It's as unlikely as . . . as . . ."

"As if I had actually won all of them? Wrong. It's statistically less likely that I would have all of the right numbers in the wrong places than it would be for me to win them all." He reached in his back pocket and placed a folded-up piece of newspaper on the bar. "Take a look for yourself. I have to take a leak."

Benny unfolded the paper and scanned over each of the lottery tickets. It was like Gumby had said. The Two-Step numbers would have won the Pick 5; the Lotto, the Mega Millions; the Pick 3s, the Lotto. Benny gulped down his last beer, grabbed the one that sat in front of Gumby's stool and gulped that one down too. He sat there shaking his head, waiting for Gumby.

"Would you have gone to work today?" Gumby said when he got back.

Benny just kept shaking his head. "I don't know what I would have done. Let's go home."

Outside of Flojo's, Benny got into his car and unlocked the passenger door for Gumby, but when he looked up, Gumby was nowhere to be seen. He got out of his car and looked over at Gumby's car in the parking lot. Gumby wasn't there. He looked out at the road and saw Gumby crossing it. Benny ran out to edge of the parking lot in front of Flojo's. "Hey, man, let me take you home. It's on the way to my house."

Gumby stopped in the middle of the road, walked back, and grabbed Benny's hand. "My friend, I don't want whatever curse is after me to get us both in a fiery accident. I'd never forgive myself. Besides, we don't know the nature of what I'm dealing with. It could be contagious. I could have already cursed you too. You have a family to think about."

"Listen, you're talking crazy," Benny said, "there's no such thing as curses."

"Benny, when the impossible happens, it's a miracle or it's a curse. This was a mathematical impossibility, and not the kind that makes you a millionaire. So I'll take my chances walking. Thank you." Then Gumby walked away.

Benny wanted to stop him, or at least to say he tried. Watching Gumby walk into the darkness that led to the streetlights of town, Benny wanted to feel bad for letting his friend walk the miles he had in front of him. He wanted to but didn't. There was enough bad luck in the world, and enough of it was already on his shoulders. So he got in his car and drove the long way around so he wouldn't have to pass Gumby on the side of the road.

When he got home, Benny instinctively opened the front door as quietly as possible but, realizing that it wasn't necessary, walked in full-footed and turned on the lights and television in his living room for company and distraction from the silence of a once-full house now empty. Not staying to watch the television, Benny took his shirt off and walked to his bedroom. When he got there, he couldn't bring himself to mess up the nicely made bed or to smell the cold pillow next to his, so he walked down the hall to his son's room.

The room was small, but the closet's folding doors had been left open, and no clothes had been left in it, opening up the room a bit. He got in the bed that was too small for him to stretch out in and looked around. He wasn't going to cry tonight. He'd done that for three nights straight. On the shelf by the window at the far side of the room, Benny saw that his son had left his baseball glove. He knew his son would be missing it, and that made him happy. He looked up at multicolored blades of the ceiling fan in the center of the room and wondered if any of Gumby's bad luck had rubbed off on him. He thought about it for a while, worrying, then fell into a deep, peaceful sleep when he realized that there was no amount of bad luck or curses that could make things any worse than they already were.

Remember, Before You Go

Joey was disappointed that J.R.'s mother was not home when he walked across the street from his house to meet up with J.R. before going out that night. He had planned on getting all of his goodbyes for the Recio family out of the way before he went out and got too drunk to say anything and sound sincere. Mr. Recio was there and, though he had never been as close to Joey as his wife had, he had a handshake and a hug to give to Joey before he left.

"Be safe over there." His words were short, but the look of respect he gave told Joey all he needed to know. Joey was no longer just the kid from across the street who was always interloping on breakfasts, dinners, and family TV hours, and to Mauricio Recio Sr. he was more than J.R.'s best friend. He was a man now, a Marine. Standing taller and straighter than he ever had, with a muscular frame and the same crew cut that had marked men as warriors when Mr. Recio was a child and his cousins and neighbors served their country against the North Vietnamese, Joey was a different person than the scared, slightly scrawny boy who had left for basic training what seemed mere days ago.

Joey excused himself from the awkward scene in the living room, where Mr. Recio had made a big deal of getting up from his La-Z-Boy to shake Joey's hand and give him a hug closer than the ones he seldom gave his own son. He went into the bathroom in the hall and let the water faucet run to drown out the silence of the bathroom and the cacophony in his head. When a couple of minutes had passed and the sink was full of water, Joey shut off the faucet and cupped some water in his hands before it all went down the drain. He rubbed the cool water on his face and behind his neck. After toweling off his face, neck, and hands, Joey thought, looking in the mirror, that he didn't look like the man Mr. Recio was looking at in the living room.

When he stepped out of the bathroom, he saw that the door to Cristela's room across the hall was slightly open. He stepped across the hall

15

quietly, so Cristela wouldn't hear him trying to look in. In all of his years of friendship with J.R., Joey had never been into Cristela's room, nor had he ever been curious as to what was in there. Walking out of the bathroom and out of Greenton, as he would be the next morning, Joey was compelled to the open door he had never been behind. He could see the foot of her bed and, on the wall, the left edge of a poster he couldn't fully see through the opening in her doorway. Making anything out in the room was made more difficult by the fact that it was lit only by a desk lamp.

Joey wanted to see more. He felt his hand rise up to the door, intending, on its own, to push it open a bit more. Before his hand touched the door, Joey heard someone walking toward the hallway from the living room. He managed to break his concentration on the room and look over to see Cristela walk into the hallway. His hand was still inches from the door when Joey spoke to her surprised smile.

"Hi, Chela. I thought you were in there. I was going to say goodbye."

Cristela was sixteen and a half years old. She had never been more than J.R.'s little sister to Joey. She had always existed peripherally in the Recio home, just as Mauricio Sr. had. But with the reality of the goodbyes he was saying opening his eyes to what he had never noticed, everything looked different to Joey. Greenton looked like a home, to be missed rather than loathed, Mauricio Sr. looked like something more than the bump on the couch he'd always been, and Cristela looked more like a woman shedding off the last few remnants of girlhood, bearing no resemblance to J.R.'s little sister.

"Thanks, Joey," Cristela said, getting closer to him and putting her arms around him. "I went to the living room to make sure I saw you before you left."

Joey stood still, his hand still up to, but not touching, Cristela's door. She squeezed him tightly and put her face on his chest.

"Can you do me a favor?" Cristela didn't pick her head up, asking her question into Joey's chest. "Can you send me a postcard from wherever they station you?"

"Well, Chela, I'm probably going to ship out right from Pendleton, and I won't see much of California outside of the base. You should have asked when I was in basic, I was pretty much right in downtown San Diego." Joey dropped his hand to his side and straightened his stance.

"Then send me a postcard from wherever you end up. I don't care. I just thought it'd be nice to know where you are, what you're seeing." When she pulled her head back to look at Joey, he noticed that Cristela hadn't been crying, as he'd thought she was. The smile on her face was a confusing one.

"Fuck it." Cristela looked away. "I don't care about postcards. I didn't ask for one when you left the first time. Just make it back here safe." The smile on her face faded away with that sentence. "My brother told me to tell you he's waiting in the car. Have fun tonight."

Joey nodded and was going to turn to leave when Cristela grabbed his arm. "Be safe," she said. She squeezed his arm, then traced it all the way down to his hand with her fingers, rubbing his hand with her thumb when it got there. Joey looked down at his hand made big and hard by its proximity to Cristela's small, delicate fingers, then up at her. He walked away from Cristela and away from her room and away from the house across the street from his own, trying to take it all in, but knowing that every moment of that night, before his friends took him out, would be devoured in his memory by the feel of Cristela's fingers on his hand and of her eyes on his before he walked away.

Flojo's was empty when Joey and J.R. walked in, except for Liz behind the bar and Vicente, her husband, shooting pool at one of the bar's two tables. Liz and Vicente looked at the boys searchingly. Joey's instincts were telling him to walk right back out of the door and go home for the night.

"Grab a couple beers," J.R. told him. "I need to take a leak."

He went to the bar and asked Liz for two beers. She was going to say something, but before she could, Vicente called to her from the pool table.

"Vieja." He spoke the way a father speaks when he knows he doesn't have to yell or apologize to anyone for anything. Liz looked at him and he gave her a nod he didn't have to explain. She rang up the beers, but again Vicente spoke up. "Give 'em a couple rounds."

Liz closed the register, gave Joey a smile, and opened the beers before she handed them to him. He took the beers to a table, but not before giving Vicente a nod that was returned with a smirk. Vicente wasn't a big man, but that didn't lessen how intimidating he was. He was wearing a black guyabera with short sleeves, the bottom of which barely covered tattoos on his arms, starched black Dickies, and a solid black pair of Stacy Adams shoes that were so polished they shouldn't have been walking on the dusty floors that he owned and his wife cleaned. He had a mustache that Pancho Villa would have envied.

The grey fedora Liz was wearing was too big for her head; it was obviously Vicente's, and the brim fell over her right eye. She looked good in the white tank top and black slacks she was wearing, though she wasn't trying to. Vicente and Liz were the kind of people no one looked at in public. They had lived in Greenton and run Flojo's since Vicente got out of prison in 1983. The wrinkles on their faces and streaks of grey in their hair hadn't detracted from their status as the toughest couple in town. Vicente put money into the jukebox. Michael Salgado sang a song about wanting only a wooden cross at his grave, and for it to be blessed with tequila when he dies.

"I thought there would be more people here," Joey said to J.R., who joined him at the table. Joey looked around, studying the room.

Flojo's had seemed so mysterious and alluring when Joey would see it as he drove past. The bar was just outside of Greenton, on the road that led to Realitos, then to Benavides, then to Alice and Corpus Christi and San Antonio and the world. Joey always saw Flojo's as a place where people get together, get drunk, have fun, and meet women. It was all of these things, not always in good ways, but Joey wouldn't see that in one night.

"C'mon, man, it's Tuesday night, and it's still early. I know we'll be seeing some unemployed drunks roll in here before the night's through." J.R. took a drink of his beer. "I just hope we don't see any of my uncles here."

J.R. was always the fastest boy in his classes throughout school. He led the Greenton Greyhounds to three regional basketball championship games. That the Greyhounds lost every championship game he played in didn't diminish J.R.'s great run as captain. He also lettered four years in a row in football and baseball. He blamed a groin injury for the fact that he did not receive any scholarship offers from colleges in any sport. The truth is that not many college scouts make it to the AA South Texas regional basketball championship game, and walking on for a squad was out of the question, because one needs to be enrolled at a school to be eligible for that.

Only a year removed from senior class, J.R. had softened greatly but still retained his slender build. Joey had always seen J.R. as the epitome of strength and masculinity. After boot camp, seeing drill sergeants and recruits and patrolmen, the biggest and baddest from their own respective hometowns, Joey lost something of the J.R. he grew up with. It was nothing big, but Joey still tried to hide it from his best friend.

Joey and J.R. were halfway through their second beers when Noe and Severiano walked into the bar, each looking as if they were playing dress-up in their fathers' clothes, wearing western shirts with nauseating patterns, tight Wranglers, and polished nothingskin boots. Joey and J.R. were both in jeans and T-shirts. A few other people had drifted in quietly before them, but Noe and Severiano threw the bar door open, shouting in unison as they came in.

"I don't know but I been told, Eskimo pussy is mighty cold!"

The drunks, who had all lined up at the bar, looked over to the door unaffected. Joey and J.R. burst into laughter, and Vicente, who was still shooting pool, shut up the loud newcomers with a stern look. Severiano apologized to Vicente as he walked to the bar, as did Noe, who clutched the neck of a bottle covered by a brown paper bag as he went to Joey and J.R.'s table.

"Four glasses and four beers, please, Lizita. It's gonna be a long night."

"Goddamn, Sevre, why you gotta be so loud?" Liz asked as she lined up four glasses on the bar. "Keep that up and we won't let you in here when you actually turn twenty-one. You guys have to lay that bottle on its side. It means you brought it from home. We aren't licensed to sell liquor."

When Severiano got to the table with the glasses and the beers, Noe was already halfway through one of his jokes.

". . . and she said, 'That's what I've been trying to tell you.' Get it?" If because of nothing more than the desperation with which Noe asked whether they understood the joke, Joey laughed and J.R. followed his lead.

"All right, all right. Now I gave my brother $40 for a bottle of whiskey, and he pitched in money to get you a bottle of Gold Label," Severiano said as he filled the glasses. "He said for you to drink one for him. He would have come but he works in the morning, and when he starts with one drink, he ain't stopping till he has to be carried home."

"Pinche Scotch. Why do you and your brother always want Scotch?" Noe said after gulping down some beer.

Severiano was filling the last glass, his, when he stopped to think about the question.

"Our Grandpa really liked Scotch. I don't even know why. When he found out he was dying, he decided, fuck it, he'd buy only good Scotch. He would always buy expensive brands, and when he really stopped giving a fuck, he would let me and my brother drink with him. I was only fourteen. They said all the booze he drank made him die faster. He wasn't even eating. But what did he want to live for, so he could get more sick and weak?"

Severiano laughed through his nose, and Noe gave a quiet "Fuck yeah." Joey and J.R. looked over at Vicente taking a shot at the pool table. Severiano filled his glass to the top, looked up, and said, "Shit, I'm not even drunk yet."

J.R., sensing the moment had passed, grabbed a glass of Scotch for himself and handed one to Joey. "Well then, let's fix that. To Joey. To his safety and protection." They raised their glasses, then emptied them.

"I seriously didn't think that you, of all the people in school, would become a goddamn jarhead," Severiano said. The mess of empty beer bottles was flirting with the edges of the table, the ashtray was near full, and only a few drunks remained in the bar.

"Yeah, bro, if I would have guessed, I would have said J.R." Noe looked at Joey and laughed. "I mean, you weren't in football in school, and you didn't get in any fights or anything. You were smart. Joining the Marines seems like more of a meathead thing to do, right, J.R.?"

J.R. had been quiet throughout the night. He let Noe and Severiano do the talking and left the laughing to Joey. Joey flicked at the filter of his cigarette with his thumb, not looking up.

"Yeah, meatheads like us." J.R. raised his palms like Christ in *The Last Supper*. "Like me."

Noe laughed and Severiano had a drink of his Scotch. Joey looked at J.R., who gave him a smile and a nod. Joey knew his best friend wasn't okay.

At the end of the night, after kicking the drunks who had come in for a Tuesday night of drinking and shooting pool out into a world where they'd have to figure out why they were jobless, broke, and lonely, Vicente and Liz let the kids who were drinking at the table in the corner of the bar stay after hours. Liz shut off all of the lights except for the neon beer advertisements and the fluorescent tubes hanging over one of the pool tables. Vicente turned down the jukebox so that no one outside would hear it. They both just sat behind the bar, smoking cigarettes, talking, and pocketing the cash the boys would give them for the beers they drank after hours.

Noe and Severiano were at the good pool table, missing shots—one or the other occasionally falling down after concentrating too hard on a left-handed shot that neither of them could have made sober. Joey and J.R. sat at the table talking about what was probably going to happen to Joey in the coming months.

"You see, I'm infantry. They're going to send me over right out of the gate." There wasn't the slightest sound of fear or worry in Joey's voice. "I'm going to ride with a light armored mobile division, which is good and bad at the same time. We'll be riding around armed with the best weapons in the world, but we'll also be the biggest targets in whatever stretch of desert we're in. I was told that I'd be there from a year to eighteen months, but I know guys who've gotten stuck over there for more than two years."

"So it's possible you won't be home for a couple of years?" J.R. sounded surprised.

"Yeah, even when I'm done, I'll probably only be stateside for a little while before I get sent out for another tour, the way this war's going." Joey knew he was being too nonchalant. He'd had months to come to terms with the fact that he was going to war; they didn't let him forget it at the recruitment depot in San Diego. It seemed J.R. hadn't seen further than Joey returning from boot camp. "Hey, I'll write home, and my mom is getting Skype. You're only going to be across the street from her. When she and I talk, you and I will talk. With me gone, you and your mom are all she has. Take care of her."

"How was she tonight?" J.R. asked.

"Oh, she's good. She was just upset that she couldn't spend the whole night with me. But I told her I needed to see you guys anyway." Joey looked at his watch. "She's going to be up any minute now to go to work."

"I've never understood going to work at four in the morning to make tortillas and empanadas," J.R. said as he finished the last cigarette in his pack.

"The dirty business of panaderias," Joey said, then finished the last of the Scotch. "Let's get out of here."

After thanking and saying goodbye to Liz and Vicente, neither of whom said more than "You're welcome" or "Goodnight," Joey convinced Severiano and Noe to let him take them home. He drove J.R.'s car to Severiano's house, where Severiano and Noe got out. Slurred goodbyes were exchanged.

"Sevre, don't let him drive yet."

"All right, Joey. You knock 'em dead."

Joey laughed, but not at Severiano's ironic well-wishing. He laughed at the thought that neither Severiano nor Noe would remember much of the night, as they had each done more than enough drinking for the whole bar.

Joey tried to appreciate every sight of Greenton as the moonlight and streetlights painted it at four-thirty in the morning. When he got out of the car at J.R.'s house, he tried to define the smell of the dry heat that he never knew he would miss until he was alienated by the salty smell of ocean air in California, and which he never feared forgetting until he learned exactly when he would have to ship out.

"So, when does your bus leave?" J.R. asked. For the first time all night, Joey heard unveiled honesty in J.R.'s voice. It revealed a sadness not to be shared in barrooms or with drunken friends who wouldn't get it.

"The bus gets to the gas station at eight, and then it's a ten-hour ride with three transfers to get to San Antonio," Joey said, not knowing how to respond to his best friend's pain. The sound of dogs barking in the distance reminded the boys that there was a world outside of the Recio driveway.

"Your mom," Joey remembered. "I didn't say goodbye to your mom."

"Let's go in, she'd be upset if she didn't see you before you left," J.R. said, appearing relieved.

"Mama." The boys had walked as slowly as possible to the bedside of J.R.'s parents, and J.R. tried to wake his mother with a whisper. "Mom," he said louder.

"What? What's wrong?" Mrs. Recio woke with a start. She looked at the clock on the dresser across the room.

"Mrs. Recio, I wanted to say bye. I'm leaving in a few hours." Joey knelt down close to Mrs. Recio so she wouldn't have to get up.

"Oh, Joey. I thought I wasn't going to get to see you. Thank you so much for waking me up." She seemed to be getting her wits about her. "You guys stink."

Joey was embarrassed. J.R. stifled his laughter so he wouldn't wake his father.

"I hope you guys had fun," she continued. "Ay mi'jito. Por favor, ten' cuidado."

"Yes, ma'am. Go back to bed. I'll write you guys." Joey gave her a hug and a kiss on the cheek. "Goodnight."

Joey led the way out of the Recio parents' bedroom, to the living room, where the front door was, reminding both him and J.R. that he was leaving. With every step he took toward the living room, J.R. right behind him, a feeling of empty weight was building in his stomach, making his head hurt and his sweaty toes tap nervously in his shoes. Joey stopped in the living room and turned around to see that J.R. was crying, his deep sobs causing his head to bob up and down.

Joey put his arms around J.R.'s shoulders, squeezing him tightly. J.R. put his head on Joey's shoulder and continued crying. Joey was quiet. He just let J.R. cry, feeling the warm tears wet his shoulder.

"It's all going to be okay. I'll be back before you know it. Just imagine I'm in jail or something."

Hearing this, J.R. stopped crying and pulled back.

"Two years, probably more." J.R. said this angrily. "You're going to be gone for two years. And what do I have? Getting drunk with Sevre and Noe in Sevre's garage? And by the time you get back, we'll be drinking at Flojo's like the borrachos that were there tonight. After high school, living here didn't seem too bad, because I knew you were going to be here with me."

"We're nineteen years old." Joey was calm. "It's a couple of years. It'll be over before you know it."

"That's supposed to be fine by me? These are going to be the shittiest years of my life, but I'm supposed to be fine by that because it's only for two years? Fuck you making it seem like it's not going to be hell."

"Well, you know what? Two years isn't a long time. I could fucking die over there. They kept reminding us of that at the depot. And you're afraid of lonely nights in Greenton? You pray for two years. That's what you should do, so bullets flying over *my* head doesn't suck too much for you." Joey turned to leave after saying this, but J.R. grabbed his arm.

"I'm just scared. I want you to be okay. I'm going to miss you, but I want you to be okay." J.R. started crying again. "Nothing here is going to matter to you in two years. It'll all be the same. Football games in the fall, baseball in the spring. Going to work every day, living in this town. But you'll be different. You left for boot camp as my friend and came back something different. With a haircut and three months of boot camp, you're not you. You talk about armor and bombs and being a target like it's nothing. What do you think three years of war will do? How much do you think you're going to care about me?"

Joey hugged him again, this time squeezing harder. "You're my best friend. I've known you forever. You are all I have outside of my mom. All I've ever had is Mom and across the street. All I'll have to miss is Mom and you."

J.R. kept crying and Joey kept holding him. His face was on Joey's shoulder, and his arms were at his sides. Joey gave J.R. a consoling pat on the back, thinking the moment was over, and released his embrace. Before Joey could take a half step back to compose himself, J.R. grabbed him in his own embrace. J.R.'s arms wrapped around Joey at his shoulders so that when J.R. dug his face into Joey's shoulder again, Joey could only hold onto J.R.'s thin torso. The wet warmth of tears on Joey's shoulder was replaced by heavy breaths punctuated by the soft rise and fall of J.R.'s chest and the now slight bobbing up and down of J.R.'s head. J.R. turned his head, planting his face into Joey's neck. Joey felt J.R.'s every breath, a cold rush falling down his spine at the feeling of the warmth on his skin.

"Please, just come back." With every one of J.R.'s syllables, Joey felt J.R.'s lips move on his neck.

Joey felt briefly again J.R.'s tears. J.R.'s embrace wasn't tight or strong, but secure and unrelenting. Joey wasn't sure if he was paralyzed by the moment or if J.R. was as strong as he'd always imagined, but, for all of his effort to pull away, Joey remained stuck there in the middle of the Recio living room. Then J.R.'s hold broke and his right hand rose to Joey's neck, his thumb and forefinger pushing ever so slightly up into Joey's hair. J.R. pulled his head back slightly to meet Joey face-to-face.

"Come back," he said, holding tight.

Joey could feel nothing but J.R.'s hand on his neck and hot breath in his face.

"All right. I should go try to get some sleep before I go," Joey said, stepping back. J.R. took a step back too and wiped his face. He looked down and J.R. looked over to the clock on the wall.

"Shit, I haven't even packed yet. I'll call you when I get to Pendleton and tell you what I can about where I'm going."

"All right." J.R. put his hands on Joey's shoulders. "You go pack. I'm going to bed."

"Okay, I'm going to the bathroom first. I'll let myself out."

J.R. nodded with a sniffle and walked to his bedroom.

Joey stood at the sink after using the bathroom and turned the faucet on halfway. He didn't want to see who would look back at him if he looked into the mirror. He felt a pain in his stomach that was more than the result of a night's worth of heavy drinking and smoking. The pain was so sharp that it had him hunched over, crying silently into the sink. He knew it would all be different when he got back, if he got back. He washed the tears from his eyes, shut off the faucet, and dried his face with a towel.

Leaving the bathroom, Joey looked across the hall at Cristela's closed bedroom door. Without hesitation or carefulness, Joey opened the door and went in. He still couldn't tell what the poster on the wall was; it was too dark in the room. He stood in the darkness, letting his eyes adjust, until he could make out a path to the wall. He walked over, quietly now but still without hesitation.

It was a horse, black, Joey thought, running across a desert—hills of sand rolling under the same sun that would beat down on Joey in his uniform, carrying his gear, spreading peace, and dodging bullets and homemade bombs.

"Joey," Chela said in a loud whisper.

Joey wondered whether he had entered the room too loudly or if she had just felt his presence in the room.

"Chela," he said quietly, trying not to scare her. "I'm sorry, I was just—" he made to point to the poster but thought better of it and headed out of the room.

"Wait, Joey, it's okay. Don't worry about it," she said, having woken up fully. "Come here." She pushed the blanket that was balled up next to her down to the floor.

Joey walked over to Chela's bedside and stood awaiting what he never would have expected to be his last goodbye in town. Chela patted the very edge of the middle of her bed. Joey sat there, trying to occupy as little space as possible.

"We got back," he said, "and I hadn't seen your mom to tell her goodbye, so I came in and woke her up." Chela sat up in bed and put her arms around Joey's chest, hugging him from behind. She had never touched him like this, but it didn't feel wrong. She was as close to a sister as anything Joey had, and tonight was a night for being regarded differently by a world about to be abandoned. "Then I was talking to your brother for a while, and now I have to go home and get ready for tomorrow."

Chela put her right hand on Joey's right shoulder and kissed the left side of his neck. Joey was paralyzed from the shock, sensory and psychic, from being where he was, feeling those lips, her lips, on his body. She pulled him down onto the bed. Joey lay looking up at Chela leaning over him, his eyes now fully adjusted to the dark. Her long hair was falling on either side of his face, making a tunnel that ended in Chela. Her lips were full like he'd never noticed; her eyebrows met in a thin trail at the middle of her forehead, like her mother's, like J.R.'s.

She kissed Joey soft on the mouth, then on his chin and neck. Joey wanted to push her off, but she was moving at such a speed that he was only able to experience her, not react to or engage her. She got on top of him and, with her left thigh, tried to nudge him to the middle of the bed.

"Wait," Joey said, catching up to where Chela's pace was taking them. It was to no avail. "Chela." He put his hands on her shoulders. "Wait, we can't. Your brother . . ."

Chela slid up to face Joey, her chest on his, her hands holding his akimbo.

"Don't worry, Joey. I won't tell him. I won't tell anyone," she said.

"It doesn't matter, Chela. It's wrong. I just said goodnight to your parents. And your brother . . ."

"But you could have this to remember when you're gone, Joey. Is it really so wrong?" Chela said, kissing Joey behind his right ear.

"Yes, it's wrong. You're like family to me. And all I'd remember is that I did your brother wrong by this," Joey said, and then gave Chela a light pat on the cheek.

"Oh, Joey," she said, letting her thighs and arms relax, collapsing down on him. She put her face on his chest, shaking her head as if trying to dig a hole in him to hide her shame. "I just thought it would be . . . I'm sorry."

"It's okay," Joey said, patting the back of her head and shhhing her rhythmically as if she were a baby. He lay there awhile, feeling Chela's breathing slow until he thought she was either asleep or faking it.

"I'm going," he whispered.

She nodded, not looking up at him. She laid her head on her pillow, and Joey picked up the balled covers she'd thrown to the ground and put them back where they were when he'd come into the room. When he opened her bedroom door, with the light creeping in from the hall, Joey could see that the horse on the poster was brown.

Joey left the Recio home quietly, locking the door behind him. He went across the street and picked up his fully packed bags. He left a note for his mother and made his way to the gas station. He got there early and sat at a booth inside, sipping a cup of coffee. When the bus got to Greenton, the town was awake and moving. People were on their way to work or play out of town. Ranchers were coming into town for breakfast after having fed their stock.

Joey put his bags under the bus and took a seat in the back. As the bus rolled out of the gas station and out of Greenton, all Joey could think about was how much he would miss J.R. and how he hoped to be missed in return.

agrosomas

"At this point in the evening, we'd like to call to the microphone a member of the Garza family to say a few words and get on with the real reason we're here tonight—you didn't all dress up just for the free food and cocktails, you know." Byron Chudley pauses here for laughter, which the audience knows to force out. "This is about Pa' Chud's generous helping of a trusted worker who had the honor, the class, to pay him back." Watching them all tap-dance on eggshells for this man who is younger than me, not even out of his thirties, I have to shake my head and smile. These are the bosses, the middle and upper management, whose asses don't go a day without being kissed either out on the ranch or in an office somewhere. They almost don't know how to pucker their lips to dole it out themselves—almost.

My father doesn't laugh, nor does he look out on, down on, the tables that fill the banquet hall in the big house of the Chudley ranch. Instead, he leans over to me and says without lowering his voice, "The chicken's dry."

"So, without further to-do, Tony Garza." Byron Chudley directs the room's attention over to our table beside the podium with his left hand. They all clap. When I get up, I have a drink of water and walk the six feet that separates me from the mic. Chudley shakes my hand, pats my back, and pulls me close to make like he has something to whisper into my ear. He actually pretends to whisper. I suppose I wouldn't have anything to say to him either if I only had a second to say it.

I stand at the podium and look out at the audience. Some of them are Chudley family members, still rich off of old cattle money and the real estate it bought the family in the early twentieth century. Some of them are relatives of executives who hit big when they suggested oil after hoof-and-mouth took out almost all of the Chudleys' livestock in the late fifties. These banquets got bigger a few years back when uranium deposits were discovered in the water table underneath much of southwest Texas. It was just something else to suckle off the Chudley teat, just another precious resource to be extracted from underneath the disc cactus, underneath the live oak and mesquite tress, inside the brown dirt that could pass for desert sand if you didn't look close enough. It was just something to add to the multibillion-dollar Chudley empire.

All of these people who buy and sell people like me, like my father, like my grandfather, on a daily basis, are watching me strut from my seat of honor to the podium and are waiting for me to speak, so that they can tear back into their dry chicken and top-shelf highballs. I almost freeze for lack of anything to say—I've never had to speak at one of these before—but I stop thinking and repeat, nearly verbatim, the words I've heard recited every year. I wave the audience's applause away.

"My name is Anthony Salinas. On behalf of the family of Alvaro Garza, and in memory of my mother, I would like to congratulate Mark Saenz of Zapata High School. It is my great pleasure, in appreciation of all of his hard work, to award him the Alvaro Garza Rural Outreach Scholarship for Outstanding Mexican American Students."

The audience gives their applause, which, probably on account of the Scotch, is a decibel or two louder than their standard golf-clapping. Byron comes back up to the podium, gives me another pat on the back, and pretends to whisper in my ear again. I take my seat, next to my father. Our work here is done.

"And I," Chudley says into the microphone, "on behalf of my grandfather, Pa' Chud, in the spirit of his legacy of kind giving and of Alvaro Garza's life of hard work and honor, I call you up, Mark Saenz, to receive your scholarship."

The kid goes up to the mic; I think I played baseball against his father back in school. He takes his big fake check, says thanks. The party and the self-congratulating can continue. As soon as the lights go down, my father and I head for the exit. We've survived yet another AGROSOMAS banquet.

"Nine hundred dollars," my father says before I have my seat belt on. "Nine hundred—" he pauses here, and I can't tell if it's for effect or because he honestly has to strain to get the word out—"*goddamn* dollars. They make it seem like he fronted $30,000 for tuition, bought linens for his bed, and gave him a jar of quarters to call home with." He said these exact words last year, except for the "goddamn," and it's his new addition, coupled with the fact that he doesn't realize he's repackaging his clever thought for new, that makes me laugh.

I stopped laughing at the bullshit of the situation when Grandpa died, and I stopped forcing a smile throughout the presentation when Mom died, but I won't stop attending them until Dad dies too, because he promised Mom he would keep going, and he made me promise he'd never have to go to an AGROSOMAS banquet alone. He says it's only that he promised her, and that's probably mostly true. But it's not just the promise that takes him to the Chudley ranch every year. It's being inside those gates and fences, where my grandfather was born and worked his whole life. It's the prospect of seeing the dirt on which so many of his stories took place. It's standing on that ground and seeing the old mesquite trees that I know I've come to associate with him, and with my father; it's breathing in the air that smells clean and unpolluted—like the past.

Alvaro Garza was not my father's father. He was just a ranch hand my dad met when he was a dropout roughneck who signed on to work setting up a rig at Chudley ranch. My father, in all of his seventeen-year-old wisdom, showed up to work hung over one day, and tried to nurse it with the dog that bit him—well, the turkey that bit him: the Wild Turkey. A few nips of the stuff in the morning on top of what he'd had the night before had my father nice and dehydrated under the Texas sun that summer day in 1960. He told me that he'd never felt anything hotter than the dirt he fell into, face-first, the day he met my grandfather.

Alvaro was out burning nopales with a blowtorch when he heard a commotion from the crew working on the rig. He drove over in his truck, an old flatbed, and told the men to put my father in the cab. He told me my father threw up three times on the floor of his truck. When my father got back to work, two days later, he gave thanks to my grandfather, who told him none were needed. The two sparked up a friendship, with Alvaro often telling the boy, Emilio, that he should go back to school. The ranch wasn't a place for someone to start his life, no matter how much money an oil company paid. Cattle didn't sustain the ranch forever, he told my dad, oil wouldn't either, and pockets made fat on sweat and sore backs don't stay that way for long. Books were the way out. He had even had a daughter who could help Emilio with his schoolwork.

My grandfather eventually talked my dad back into school, and my mom helped him graduate. My grandfather made sure my father's stay at Chudley ranch was no longer than a summer, and, to hear my father tell it after a few beers, he saved his life—gave him one. When we get to the front gate of Chudley ranch, I cut off my headlights and turn left onto a dirt path inside the ranch. I take the path slowly, riding the brake and letting the sound of brush scratching on either side of the truck guide me to our destination.

When we get to the gate, my father gets out and signals for me to give him light so he can work the numbers on the combination lock. He turns around, smiling in my headlights, gives me a thumbs-up, and then, slashing at his throat with his hand, tells me to cut the lights again.

"I knew it! I just knew they wouldn't change the damn locks." He pounds excitedly on the dashboard and laughs like a kid. I've never seen him like this. "It's three and a half miles up. Take it slow, mi'jo."

While my family came into being at Chudley ranch, the place has come to represent the best and worst of our past, like any home. My grandfather was born here in 1923, when the closest doctors to be found were in Kingsville, Alice, Laredo, or the ranches. He went to school here and worked here his whole life because it was, as he called it, his ranch—our ranch. I listened, fascinated, as a kid, to his stories of my ancestors, his grandparents or his parents' grandparents, who owned Chudley. The vaqueros, he told me, broke the horses and herded the cattle in Texas before it was even called that. They loved the job so much, he said, that they stuck around to do the job after the split from Mexico. They did it for the horses and the cattle—for the land.

It took my uncle, Alvaro Jr., home from college the year I turned ten, telling me that the Garzas never owned or ran Chudley ranch, to dispel for me the myth my grandfather had made. He talked about Aztlan and revolutions and coercive land contracts and how even the land his parents' home was on, land that they owned outright, wasn't really theirs.

"They can park a house there," he said, "but if they ever hit oil, they might as well burn it. No one owns the rights to anything in their soil. The Chudleys do. The Joneses and the Kings do too. We just break our backs so they can make more money." Three years into a college education, and my uncle could already crush a child's illusions and lay claim to labor he never did. Pa' Chud would be happy that his money had done so much good.

"This is it," my father says when we pull up to the oil pump. Driving through southwest Texas, one can take for granted the size of a rotating oil pump up close. No one but a roughneck, my father will say when he sees one, knows what goes into getting that pump up. "Hard to tell if it's still producing as much as it used to, but in its prime it made Pa' Chud some money. We had the derrick up that summer. When I quit for school, they were already drilling." He steps slowly onto the service platform and inspects the valves and gauges on the pump. "I came back that summer and on school holidays that year, and every year during college."

I look around at the site and try to imagine my father working like my uncle never had to, like I never did. Watching him examine the pump, dragging his fingers across its mechanisms, I see him with a wrench and a rubber hammer, tightening valves and pounding pipes to submission. I can see him fighting to beat the earth, making the Chudleys more money they didn't need.

"Those summers, I would ride to the ranch with your grandfather. He'd get me at five in the morning every day. The summer between junior and senior year, I asked if I could marry your mother. He didn't say a word to me when I did. Hell, he never said much of anything anyway. We stopped at the bunkhouse, and I helped him load a couple bales of hay and some feed. He was silent the whole time. We rode out and when he dropped me here at the rig, he told me: Salinas, if you can keep her away from here—"

"She's yours if she'll have you for hers," I finish his sentence. He nods his head silently, not looking away from the pump.

"We had a Christmas tree up by the end of that summer. Let me tell you, if you have a chance to see a rig when the Christmas tree is up, you're just shocked someone could be so smart as to engineer a machine that well." Derricks and Christmas trees and oil pumps, blowout preventers and steam-feeders, I've taken Oil Drilling 101 more times than I can count. I just appreciate it more now.

"I kept your mom away from here, from this—" he points to the pump—"but nothing could keep her from this ranch, or from Greenton, for that matter. She learned to ride here, on Chudley horses. And your grandfather wouldn't leave either. He came up with Pa' Chud, knew him when he was just a snot-nosed, cattle-rich brat. He'd gotten his annual bonuses and was sent home with a turkey every Thanksgiving and a ham every Christmas. Why wouldn't he think to ask for a loan to cover the last $900 of your uncle's tuition?"

He motions for me to come to him and help him down from the service platform. When I do, I can feel how light he is, how fragile—like I can just crush him to dust if I don't take care not to. He walks away from the pump and looks out at the lights coming from the house.

"Me and your mom, we just went to A&I. Half the people in town who go to college do. But your uncle went all the way out to College Station. It ran a little more. It wouldn't have taken five years for your grandfather to pay back if Chud hadn't changed the interest rate so many times.

It was that he got into the polvo real bad for a while, and you can't cut company checks for that stuff. The damn thing had to have been paid off about four times when all was said and done. Did your grandfather complain once? No. He even showed up to the banquets, sat up on that platform, on display, so Pa' Chud, then JR, and now Byron Chudley, could show their hunting buddies the poor Mexican they did right by."

The air is fresh out here in the middle of the ranch, fresh but not cold. Still, I find myself shaking—shivering in my stomach, not my back.

"I know, Dad, but he had to think it all mattered for something. That it wasn't just a big run-around. He had to believe that this place he gave his life to had actually given him something back. It certainly wasn't the money, and maybe that's why Pa' Chud started the damn thing, to do right by him." I lean back on the service platform, the shivering having gotten worse.

"Do you really think that?" My father turns to face me. "Like your mother did? That any part of it was actually for him?"

"No, and I don't think she did either. But he did, and that's enough for me."

"That's exactly what she used to say. Those exact words."

He's right. Tonight, I've repeated two of my mother's speeches. I nod.

"And if those words were good enough for her," I say, "then they're enough for me."

My father stands silent, looking at me, wanting to fight but knowing that, like he couldn't against her, he can't win this one. He walks to the platform, looks at the stars in the sky, and then begins to walk away. When he gets so far away that I can't hear the dirt crunch under his boots, I go after him. When I catch up to him, he's crouched down with his palm on the ground.

"There are sixty head of cattle buried here. Right here, they dug a pit in '57, and buried sixty head of cattle." He looks around at the ground. "When I got here in '60, you could still see the outline of where the pit was buried. It was big like you wouldn't believe."

I look down at the ground and can't imagine how big it would have to have been.

"Hoof-and-mouth came up big and bad from across the border. They had makeshift chutes that led the cattle here and then 'pop,' like that, with a rifle. That's only a fraction of what they lost. Your grandfather took turns with two other cowboys pulling the trigger. They'd shoot them and hope they fell over into the pit; if not, they'd all have to push. Sixty head. Then they doused the lot of 'em in gasoline, struck a match, and let it burn all night. The next morning they poured lye in the pit and filled it back up. He said it was the worst thing he'd ever smelled in his life.

"I asked him, joking, if it wouldn't just smell like barbecue. Let me tell you, I've never seen him so cold. He said him and the other cowboys puked. They puked their guts up and they cried their eyes out. These men whose job it was to care for and nurture animals so they could be slaughtered, they all cried their eyes out at having just killed and burnt sixty head of cattle. They don't have an annual dinner and give out scholarships for his work on this fucking ranch. No, they have it because he paid back money he'd made for Pa' Chud in the first place. I want you to think about every day in your life that you knew your grandfather and count the times you saw him cry, and I want you to tell me if this circus should be enough. It's not enough for him and it's not enough for your mom and it's not enough for me. It shouldn't be enough for you."

He gets up and looks at me face-to-face.

"It's not, but you promised Mom—"

"I know I did, and you promised me. But don't you ever forget that it's not enough. Hell, the man couldn't eat meat for quite some time after that."

"Dad, I never ate a meal with Grandpa when he wasn't eating meat."

"Well, shit, I know that. But who doesn't eat meat?" he tells me and we walk back to the car.

I drive us back to the gate, and my father says he's tired, so he tells me the combination for the lock. I get out and flip the digits in place. I open it up, get in the car to pull it forward, and get out to close it behind us. We get to the main gate, and I look back at big house where the banquet has turned into a party like it does every year.

"This drink is for Alvaro Garza," I say, mocking Byron Chudley's deep voice and drawl, "the best sonuvabitch I never met but who my pappy said was a good enough man to get dressed up and loaded for, a man who worked on my ranch doing stuff to things with other things."

"The man whose ranch I own," my father says. He laughs deep and hard and slaps at the dashboard. "You know, I don't think he knows how to ride a horse."

I laugh at this as I turn on 281 to get us home. "Really? Where'd you hear this?"

"Mando Lugo, the *cuate,* the fat one, he works at the uranium plant out here, and he said he'd seen him ride out here on a jeep, pulling a horse in a trailer to move to another stable. When the jeep broke down, he called to the uranium plant, which he was pretty close to, so they could send a truck out to get him. He sat in the truck while the workers, Mando included, hitched the trailer to their truck and didn't say a word all the way to the stable."

I laugh with him, almost to the point of crying. "I guess that's what you get when you send your kid to school in Paris and college in New England."

My father slaps the dashboard again and shakes his head, smiling. In the silence that follows, I think of how glad I am that we went to the banquet and that he took me to the rig. I still can't help but hurt for my grandfather and miss my mother. This land really is ours. It's our home. I look over at my father, who is fighting sleep. He'll be out in minutes. Tomorrow, I'll call my daughter at school. I'll ask her how she's doing and if she needs anything of me. I'll tell her to make sure to call her grandfather, even though I know I don't have to. She knows we don't have too much time with him. I hope he lasts past when she graduates, so I can make her promise that, for as long as I live, I'll never have to go to an AGROSOMAS banquet alone.

The Art of Making Something out of Nothing

Memo stole the car, a white Oldsmobile 88 with holes in the floorboards and a tape of conjunto music stuck in the tape deck, from Evangelo, a punk-bitch we used to beat the shit out of in school, out of spite.

"Man, fuck him," he said as he turned on the car with the keys he had taken from Evangelo's house when Evangelo was distracted. "A brick of yay falls in his lap, and he thinks he's Tony fucking Montana."

We didn't believe Evangelo was sitting on a brick of coke when Victor, Memo's little sister's boyfriend, came up to Memo's porch, interrupting Memo's and my mid-afternoon blunt, and told us.

"All that bitch is holding is his dick." I smiled when Memo said this, but Victor laughed deep and hard. Memo didn't hold back in conveying his disgust at Victor's desperation, staring silence, shame, and a reason to leave the porch into him.

But when Evangelo called me at four in the morning, asking if Memo and I wanted to make a big purchase, I realized three things: 1. The rumor was true. 2. Memo and I had a big payday coming to us. 3. Evangelo was coked out of his mind. I answered my phone, still half asleep. All I said was "What?" and he went off, without even asking to make sure it was me who had answered the phone.

"I was visiting my uncle in Falfurrias, well, just outside of Falfurrias, mowing his lawn 'cause he's all old and can't do shit like that anymore, so my mom pays me to go visit him and cut his yard and get him groceries every week. So I'm mowing the lawn, all tired and hot and shit, and a big van stopped in front of the house. My uncle's house is right on the side of Highway 281. It was one of those fifteen-passenger vans. You know, like the church ones but not from a church. The driver of the van was yelling at the people in back, and then this chick who was sitting in the front seat threw a package out the window, into the grass ditch in front of my uncle's yard. So they sat there arguing, not even caring or knowing that I was watching them. Then the van took off like a goddamn bat out of hell. Before I could even guess what was going on, two border patrol trucks and a highway patrol car were chasing the van. I picked up the package, realized what it was, and drove it back to Corpus—not telling anyone and not driving over sixty my whole way home. I was so fucking scared, Kiki." Evangelo breathed hard on the other end of the line, waiting for my reply.

"What the fuck are you talking about?" I knew who it was, but I didn't understand why he was calling me. "No one calls me Kiki anymore, it's Rick."

"It's Evangelo, Evangelo Quintero. It was coke, Rick. It was a whole brick of coke." He was giddy when he said this, and I was listening, wide awake.

When I told Memo about my phone conversation with Evangelo, he was as excited and cautiously suspicious as I was. I told him how I could hear the tail end of a three-day bender on the other end of the line. Memo decided we would have to take every precaution to make sure we didn't get hurt or fucked over by some randomly fortunate loser who had been skimming lines off the top of our big paycheck. He loaded the .22 he kept in his sock drawer and enlisted the services of Mase Scranton.

Mase was this big, bad-looking black dude who looked crazy enough to get stupid but was actually too smart to get dumb. He sold dimes and nickels for us to the white kids on the south side and on the black ends of the cuts where some people, mostly hardcore bangers and old-timers, weren't too keen on buying weed from the little chavalos who sold for us in our neighborhood. Mase was always real loyal to Memo and me, and Memo knew we would need his help to distribute and collect the money from the coke we would soon be selling.

Mase went to Miller back in the day, where he knew a cousin of mine. He was all books and football and basketball back then. He'd gotten a scholarship to UTSA, but came home when his dad got sick, and stayed here because Corpus seems to do that to you.

There was another, more immediate benefit in promoting Mase to partner. He was, as I said, a "big bad brotha" and, despite how many asskickings we'd thrown Evangelo's way over the years, we wanted to make sure we could intimidate him with some muscles and a hard face he didn't know from Black Adam when we showed up at his place.

We had already established a system that worked for selling the weed we would get from Memo's uncle, a truck driver who had drug connections through Texas down to Mexico. Evangelo knew this, hence his calling us at four in the morning. Well, he called me specifically. He was probably too scared to call Memo.

Tuesday night, the night it was all going to go down, Memo bought a case of beer and rolled a blunt. The beer was to celebrate after the deal, and the blunt was for us to smoke beforehand, to calm our nerves. The three of us met at Memo's at midnight and strategized over a few cold ones and the blunt. At two o'clock, the time he specified, we walked to Evangelo's house, which is just down the street from Memo's, with Mase, Memo's loaded .22, and a wad of cash in a backpack. When we got there, something unexpected but not too surprising happened—the fucker stonewalled us.

"I want ten thousand. I won't take anything less than ten grand." I had just closed the front door to Evangelo's house behind me when he made his prepared statement. I was almost impressed by Evangelo's declaration, but when I took a good look at him, I realized he wasn't trying to play hardball. He was just fried beyond sensibility. He was bug-eyed and sweating, and he smelled like it was the brick that found him in a ditch and not the other way around.

"Whoa, calm down. We don't get a 'hi' or nothing like that?" I don't know who I was trying to calm down—Evangelo, who had to chill out, or Memo, who I knew wouldn't put up with too much bullshit from anyone, much less from the clown who was dishing it out right then. Memo was mad-dogging Evangelo something mean, but Evangelo wouldn't look back at him. He kept the small blacks of his bloodshot eyes fixed on me, breaking his concentration to sneak quick, confused, suspicious glances at Mase.

"Ten grand or no deal." Evangelo fixed his stare back on me.

"Fuck ten grand. We ain't even seen what we're buying." Memo had stressed the first sentence. "Where is it?"

Evangelo looked like he was answering a riddle. He didn't seem to like the idea of us getting our hands on the coke before he got his on some money. He sat thinking, still looking in my direction, but now looking beyond me. I bobbed my head up to get his attention. When he was back with me, I nodded my head, trying to be as reassuring as possible. Without saying anything, he got up and left the room.

Memo looked at me and whispered, angry, "Who the fuck does he think he is? Who does he think we are?" I shrugged, not knowing what to say. Mase shook his head as if disapproving of how it was all going down.

Evangelo came back to his dirty living room and put a cardboard box that had once held a DVD player on his coffee table after kicking off empty beer cans and fast food wrappers and bags. He looked down at it and then back at me. Memo, Mase, and me all stepped forward, heads perked up to see what Evangelo had to show us. He opened the box, showing us what we were buying. The plastic-wrapped brick sat on unwrapped butcher paper. The plastic was slit open—Evangelo had been drawing from it for three days. It wasn't as big as I thought it would be, but it was still bigger than any amount of weed we'd ever sold at one time. That's how big a step up we were taking.

Memo leaned forward and reached a hand into the box.

"Nah, nah, nah, man. Ten grand." Evangelo shook his head and brushed Memo's hand away from the box, then pushed its flaps closed.

"Motherfucker, I will kill you if you touch me again. Did you forget who you're dealing with? Look at me. Snap the fuck out of it. Something fell in your lap. That's it. Don't forget who you are. You're not in Falfurrias. You're back in Corpus. I'll shoot you right now if I have to." Evangelo leaned back when Memo told him this. Memo stood, fists clenched at his sides, staring up at Evangelo. It was a funny sight, but one I'd seen many times— Memo, small and skinny as he is, even shorter than me, stepping up to someone bigger than him. Evangelo was almost as tall and big as Mase, but soft. "Now I'm going to try this to make sure you aren't dicking us around."

Memo opened the box and put some coke on his gums. He tightened his lips, went back into the box and snorted a bump. "Either he's too smart to fuck with us or too dumb to know how. We're good."

"Now, about the price . . . I think," I started.

"I want ten grand," Evangelo said, cutting me off.

"Shut the fuck up. Don't interrupt," Memo snapped at him, giving me a chance to speak.

"There's no way you can move this much weight. You'll either kill yourself or get killed 'cause you can't keep your mouth shut. We'll give you four."

"Listen, Kiki, I mean Rick, I know ya'll are going to make at least thirty grand off of this. I won't take anything less than ten." Evangelo sat down on the couch he had probably picked up off a sidewalk and set the box next to him.

"No." Memo was madder than he'd been all night. "You've had your fun. You got at least a gram, if not more. But you know what? The going rate for blind fucking luck is $4,000."

We knew that ten grand was a more than reasonable price. Hell, it was a steal. But we didn't have ten grand, we'd only brought six. We were bargain-bin thieves. Evangelo himself knew he couldn't move that much weight. But still, he stonewalled us. He demanded his ten grand.

After a long, frustrating debate, Evangelo took $5,000. He decided on that figure when Mase, who had otherwise been a silent presence in the room during the negotiations, got fed up and put his fist through Evangelo's living room wall. We had shown up with $6,000 in a backpack and walked away with a grand in change, a brick of coke (short a gram or two), and the keys to an Oldsmobile 88, which Memo had pocketed, out of spite, during Mase's show of strength and frustration.

None of us, Evangelo included, had ever made a deal that big. We had a brick of coke we'd purchased at an 84 percent discount, and Evangelo, for his trouble, got a three-day coke binge and $5,000 for a brick of coke he didn't have to work to get. Mase and I would gladly have walked back up the street to Memo's house backward and blindfolded, but when we got to the end of Evangelo's yard, Memo showed us what he'd stolen. He looked at the keys and then at Evangelo's car parked on the street in front of his house, and before Mase and I could stop laughing, we were in the car, Memo was speeding away, and the radio was blaring conjunto music through the car's cracked speakers.

The drive from Evangelo's house to Memo's took only a couple of minutes.

"All right, guys, let's call it a night," Mase said and made to get out of the car.

"Hold on, bro. We gotta celebrate," I said, fired up by the excitement of our successful business deal and the genius of Memo's grabbing Evangelo's keys. I wasn't ready for the night to end, and Memo wasn't either.

"Yeah, Mase, this is too big to go to bed and dream about. Ya'll sit tight." Memo got out of the car, its engine still running, and ran inside. He came back out with the case of beer we'd started earlier. I don't think he wanted us to end our night drinking and smoking in his garage—having to be quiet enough to not wake his mother before work or his sister before school. When he got in the car, he handed Mase and me a beer each and opened one up for himself.

"Let's hit up the beach," he said after his first sip of beer.

"Fuck yeah," I said, happy to make a night of the early morning. Memo put the car in gear and headed for the freeway.

"Wait a minute, man. Wait one goddamn minute," Mase said looking back at the distance growing between Memo's house and us. "Let's leave the shit here." He pointed his thumb behind us. "We shouldn't be driving around with this much weight on us."

"Mase, my man," I said. "You need to chill the fuck out. Ain't shit happening to us but beers, blunts, and a line or two."

"Just beer and blunts," Memo corrected me. "We stay away from the yay. And he's right." He looked over at Mase in the passenger seat. "Tonight we're untouchable."

"Nah, man, you need to go back," Mase said.

"Too late." Memo laughed like he was playing keep-away. "We're at the freeway."

"Fuckin' asshole," Mase said. He shook his head for a second, and then just leaned back in his seat.

I expected Memo to take a right when we got to the freeway, getting on going toward the harbor and Corpus Christi Beach. When he drove through the underpass and took a left, I knew he was going toward Padre Island, to J. P. Luby Beach. From Memo's house, the drive to Luby would take about thirty-five minutes. I kicked back on the backseat, sipping on a beer and looking out the window as we passed restaurant row, then the malls, then the bait-and-tackle shops, and then drove into darkness.

The city was behind us, and we welcomed the smell of the saltwater coming up from under the causeways and bridges we drove on. Mase, shaking his head again and muttering to himself, rolled a joint from a nickel bag of weed he had in his shirt pocket, lit it, and, after a while, passed it back to me. The windows were rolled down, drowning out the sounds of a smoky-voiced singer crying out songs about drinking, over accordions and twelve-string guitars.

Memo asked Mase to hold his beer. He sat up straight in his seat, scooted forward, and reached toward his lower back. When Mase saw Memo pull the .22 out of his belt strap, he dropped the roach he was sucking at onto his lap. Mase picked the roach up from his lap and threw it out his window. I took a deep, long drink from my beer.

"What the fuck are you doing?" Mase asked.

"You guys think I can shoot out a streetlight? I mean, how much do you think I'd have to slow down to hit one?" Memo put the gun on his lap and took his beer from Mase.

Mellowed out and buzzing by this point, I ventured a guess. "Fifty-five if you were sober but, right now, probably twenty-five or thirty."

"Are you nuts, man? Do you know how many felonies we're committing right now? My daddy always told me, you break one law at a time.

If you're drunk when you're driving home, don't be smoking a joint too. If there's a body in your trunk, don't speed. And if you're smoking weed, drinking beer, and carrying a fucking brick of yay, you don't shoot an unlicensed handgun out the window of the stolen car you're driving." Mase wasn't yelling out of anger, but to be heard over the rush of air coming in the open windows. He didn't necessarily seem calm either. "Besides, we're about to get to the island."

"Calm the fuck down. It ain't even loaded," Memo lied and slid the gun under his seat.

We rolled through the island at the speed limit and with the radio turned down. When we turned onto the dark road that leads to the beach, Memo turned the radio back up, and I cracked open a new beer. Though we were in the clear, we remained silent.

Living as close to the beach as we do, it's really nothing special to us. There is nothing between us and the water. We're not tied to it like we are to our streets. There are two or three blocks in the city that define Corpus as a beach town in postcards. Those blocks aren't ours. As much as we ignore and are not a part of the shoreline in the city, at least it's known territory. We've all been to the parks and taken dates for walks on the piers and visited friends and family members in the hospital across from the shore. But this place, the island, we're outright aliens here. When it's populated, this place has a way of making anyone like us, even those who aren't committing felonies, feel like criminals. Sitting in the back of the car, the stereo now just ignorable background noise, I couldn't help but feel we should have celebrated quiet and calm in Memo's garage.

Memo put both of his hands on the steering wheel and concentrated on driving on the sand that was compacted and hardened by cars that had driven on it earlier. He parked the car twenty yards from the shore, behind a wooden lifeguard stand. "It's a damn nice night for a picnic," he said and got out of the car.

It was just after three o'clock in the morning. I wasn't drunk yet, but I was far from sober. We climbed the lifeguard stand, which was big enough to seat all three of us comfortably, but closer than any of us wanted. I sat in one corner and Mase in the other; Memo stood on the sand in front of us, resting his beer on the highest rung of the ladder up to the stand, which was only six feet up. He seemed too excited to sit anyway.

"All right, we need to break the coke up. If we sell halves, quarters, and eight-balls, we'll make the most money. We can sell bigger amounts for cheaper, but we need to talk about it before we do. The real money is in selling smaller amounts. So we only sell wholesale amounts to friends and if, for some reason, we want to get the coke off our hands." Memo was animated. He paced about and flailed his arms like he was trying to fill us with the Holy Ghost. "When there ain't too much of the brick left, we can consider cooking rocks with what's left."

"I don't know, Memo. No matter how simple it is to cook, if we fuck it up, we can hurt or kill people." Memo stopped pacing when I said this.

"Shit, man, I only got B's in chemistry," Mase said.

"Yeah, and if we fuck up cooking the batches, we'll lose that much money." Memo nodded to himself, then continued pacing.

"Well, how're we going to split the profits?" Mase sat up when he asked this. In the pause that followed, he finished his beer in a gulp, crushed the can, and threw it onto the sand.

"You'll get the same percent of the profit you get when you sell weed." Memo sounded unsure.

I spoke up. "Plus a percentage of the whole profit we get from the brick. We'll talk how big later, but you can get it every Sunday when we calculate how much we got from that week."

Memo looked at me, annoyed.

"He helped us get it," I said in my own defense.

"Shit, man, we could have at least tried to haggle a little. You can't negotiate for shit." Memo said this, then dropped his empty beer can to the ground and pulled another out of the quickly emptying case.

"A brick falls in your lap, and you think you're Tony fucking Montana, or what?" Mase said. We all laughed.

"I'll drink to that," Memo said, still high off the thrill of our plan succeeding. "What're you going to do with all the money? It'll be a lot more than any chunk of change we've ever pulled down."

"I want to get out of Corpus. This place feels like it's dying." Mase lit the pinhair joint he'd rolled with the last of his weed while Memo was preaching. He offered it to me, but I declined, so he handed it to Memo. "I have a cousin who had to leave Houston because of some gang shit, and he ended up in North Dakota. The way he describes it, it sounds nice."

"Shit, man, there ain't any black people in North Dakota. You'll get hung or some shit like that." I expected Mase to laugh at my joke, but he didn't.

"Nah, the town's small and all the people care about is if you work and if you're a good neighbor. My cousin said there's actually a few Puerto

Ricans up there. You know everyone, everyone knows you. No bullshit and no hating." Mase sucked down hard on the joint he'd gotten back from Memo, leaving only a tiny roach that Memo didn't want when it was offered to him.

"And you?" Memo asked me.

"I don't know, man. Give my mom some of it. Buy some clothes for my sister. I guess I could go back to school, but it's been so long that I'd feel all old. I'd need to have it in my hand to know what I'd do with it. I'd probably do some stupid shit, though, like buy a car with a bumpin' system and rims. What about you, Scarface?"

I could see that Memo liked it when I called him that. "I'll do what any smart hustler does, reinvest that shit."

"What, like buy a shitload of weed, or more coke?" Mase looked down at Memo, who was looking out at the water.

"Definitely more coke. It's smart money. And I wouldn't keep it in town. You can get two times as much money for coke up north. I'll get my hands on as much as I can through one of my uncle's connections and take a trip to New York or Chicago or some shit like that." Seeing how high Memo had gotten off the score, I knew he was serious.

I grabbed a beer and took a drink. I wished I'd hit that last joint Mase rolled.

"Well, mister criminal mastermind," Mase said. "What's your big plan for that piece-of-shit car you stole?"

Mase looked at me, and I shook my head to tell him it was Memo's problem.

"I don't know, I guess I'll park it around the block and throw his keys in his backyard," Memo said. "He shouldn't have fucked with us."

A case of beer never lasts as long as you want it to. At five in the morning, we were out of beer. Neither Memo nor Mase were high anymore. We were all just drunk and tired. We stumbled to the car. Mase got in the backseat and lay across it trying to sleep. Memo got in the passenger seat without asking if I was okay to drive. I turned the car on, put it in drive, and took off. I didn't know where I was going.

"You're going the wrong way, we came from back there," Memo said after a while, pointing behind us.

"Oh shit, you're right." I jerked the wheel, swinging the car around. When the car was facing the right direction, I hit the gas too hard, and the wheels began to spin, digging into the sand. I kept my foot down and played with the steering wheel, but it didn't matter, we were stuck.

"Memo." I looked over at him, but he was already asleep. Realizing this was a good enough reason to rest for a while, I turned the car off and leaned back in my seat. I figured we could find something to put under the tires when the sun came up. My mind raced for a while, but the rhythmic sound of the waves rolling in and the salty sweet smell of the beach lulled me to sleep soon enough.

Memo and I woke when Mase kicked the back of the bench seat we were slouched on. "We have to leave," he told us.

"What the fuck?" Memo asked, not happy about having been woken up with a kick.

"We have to go. Look over there." Mase pointed behind us. Across the beach a small group of people in orange safety vests were making their way toward us, trash bags in hand. A sheriff's deputy was bringing up the rear.

"Shit, let's go," Memo said, rubbing his eyes. "Why did we stay here anyway?"

I turned the car on and sat as the engine warmed up. I pulled out my phone to check the time. It was almost ten in the morning. I put the car in drive, tried to take off, and remembered why I'd decided to go to sleep.

"Ah, fuck. We're stuck. That's why I went to sleep. We're stuck." I put my head on the steering wheel.

"You're shitting me. We're stuck in the middle of an empty beach, and we got a cop coming toward us?" Memo looked at the people who were approaching. "We're fucked."

"What do we do?" Mase asked.

"All right, we've got at least five minutes before they get here, because they're picking up trash. You guys get out and try to push. If we get out, we roll. If not, just make sure you get in the car before the cop gets to us. I'll take care of it then." I looked at the guys. Mase looked skeptical, Memo looked mad. "Trust me."

Mase got out of the car and positioned himself to push. Memo looked at me and shook his head. He leaned over toward me and reached under the seat. I gave him a push. He looked at me angry and in disbelief. He reached down again, and I said, "No. Just leave it. It's not even there, man." He stared at me for a second, got out of the car, and slammed the door behind him.

"You guys ready?" I asked Mase and Memo. They both nodded and I gunned the engine. The tires spun, kicking sand in their faces. They pushed down on the trunk of the car, trying to force friction between the tires and the sand. The car didn't move. Memo stood on the bumper and bounced up and down while Mase pushed forward on the car. Nothing. This continued for a while as the cleanup crew made their way toward us. I could see the deputy watching us. He seemed more amused than concerned.

I shut the engine off and Mase and Memo got in the car.

"What now?" Mase asked as he moved the backpack with our money and our investment to the floor of the backseat.

"Let me talk when he gets here," I said. Memo didn't speak. The cleanup crew wasn't too far behind us, so I put my phone up to my ear. "Yeah . . . yeah . . . mm hmm . . ." I looked back at the deputy, who was walking ahead of his group toward us. As he got closer, I really turned on the bullshit. "I know it's early, but we're stuck. . . . Yeah, out here at Luby. . . . Just come get us." The deputy was standing right behind the car now. "All right, call me when you get to the island. Bye." I put my phone in my pocket and turned around to face the deputy.

"Morning, gentlemen. Looks like you dug her in deep." He raised his sunglasses to get good looks at all of us.

"Yessir, we can't seem to make this heap budge." I stressed the "yessir," making it sound as Texan as possible, trying to highlight our similarities, and flashed him an embarrassed smile.

"What are ya'll doing out here anyway? Ya'll sleep out here?" He looked right at me.

"Yessir, we came out here to have a little going-away party for Mason," I gestured back to Mase. "We weren't planning on camping out, but I had a little too much to drink and didn't feel safe taking off. So we slept on the beach."

The deputy stood up straight and looked at the car, then at Mase. He leaned down and poked his head in my window. "Where's Mr. Mason going?"

"North Dakota," Mase said from the backseat.

"North Dakota? I got some people up in North Dakota. Whereabouts in North Dakota are you going?" The deputy took a step back and leaned to look at Mase. I suddenly felt naked in my clothes. I felt like the jeans I wore were too baggy, like the T-shirt Mase wore was cut too long, and like the tattoo across Memo's right forearm spelled the word *thug*, rather than his name.

I could feel the deputy judging us, and I knew all he could see was criminals. This time he was right.

"Hatton, sir," Mase said.

"Hatton, North Dakota." The deputy gave a laugh. "I know where that is, my people are in Grand Forks. Why would anyone want to move to Hatton?"

"I have a cousin up there who says it's nice. He's getting me a job in the potato factory. It pays well enough, and rent is cheap. I figure it'll be quiet time for me, and I'll save some money while I figure out what I want to do. It seems like a good deal." Mase looked up at the officer, who nodded his head.

"That sounds better than getting trashed at the beach on a Tuesday night," the deputy said to all of us. "You guys in front have names?"

"My name is Enrique, sir. People call me Rick," I said. "And this is—"

"Memo. My name is Memo." Memo looked in the direction of the deputy and held up his forearm to show the tall, narrow letters of his name but didn't make any further attempt at politeness.

"What was that? Is that some kind of nickname?" the deputy asked.

"It's short for Guillermo," I told him.

"Oh, like Willie," the deputy said. I nodded. "So, Rick, you have a license and proof of insurance?"

"Yessir. Let me get that for you." I reached for my wallet and motioned for Memo to look in the glove box for proof of insurance I wasn't sure he'd find.

Memo didn't make a move for the glove box; instead he spoke to the deputy. "Officer, are they supposed to be smoking?" He pointed back at the people in orange vests, a few of whom, two women and a man, were smoking. Another man was sitting, and another woman was on a cell phone.

The deputy turned around and started shouting at his cleanup crew. "Goddamn it, this is not a vacation. You're not here to get a tan and play volleyball. Put out those cigarettes and turn off that phone, or it's mine. Get over here now!" The crew started slowly for the car.

"Here's my license and I can grab the proof of insurance for you, sir." I held my card out to the deputy.

"Don't worry about it, Rick. Let's just get you out of this sand. Come here!" he yelled at his crew.

"Sir, that isn't necessary. I called my cousin and he's going to bring his truck to tow us out," I told him.

"Well, you can call him back and tell him not to come, we'll get you out." The deputy looked at his crew. "Won't we?" Nobody in the crew said anything. "Are you boys going to help us push?" The deputy looked into the car. Mase and Memo got out and went to the back of the car. "No, I think Mr. Memo should drive. He's the smallest, makes sense." The deputy pronounced the name funny—two hard syllables, stressing the "O." I got out of the car and left the door open for Memo.

Four of the cleanup crew members had their hands on the top of the car's trunk. Mase, me, and another guy had our hands under the bumper. The car was wide, but it was still crowded behind the trunk. "All right, Mr. Memo, give her gas." The deputy stood, arms crossed, watching us push the car up and over the holes the wheels had dug in the sand. When he had the car out of the sand, Memo pulled away from the shore, onto the harder sand near the dunes. He put the car in park and waited for us to get in.

"Thank you for your help, officer," I said.

"Deputy," he corrected me. "Deputy Neal. No problem, Mr. Rick. Good luck in Hatton, Mr. Mason. I hope you figure out where you're going."

"Thank you, sir. You too," Mase said, walking toward the car.

When we got in the car, Memo did a U-turn and drove slowly until we were out of sight of Deputy Neal, then he sped up. "You get the car stuck and you get a fucking sheriff's deputy on our asses?" Memo didn't look at me when he said this.

"I got us unstuck and I got him off our asses, didn't I?" I answered. "And anyway, you're going the wrong way. We came from back there."

"Oh really, you want me to go back in the direction your friend is going in? Where we left about twenty beer cans in the sand? You want a vest so you can help your buddy pick up our beer cans? We'll find a way out of the beach this way." He sped up more. "'Mr. May-Mo.' Dickhead."

Mase sat up in back and put the backpack in the seat next to him. I stayed slouched down but put my hand on the dashboard as calmly as I could.

"First Evangelo tries to fuck us over, and then deputy dickhead fucks with us because of this piece-of-shit car." Memo was talking to himself. "And how the fuck do we get out of here?"

I couldn't help it, I started laughing. Memo looked over at me. He wasn't angry, just thrown off by my laughter. "You complain more than anyone I know. I mean more than any of my grandparents or anyone. Seriously, we got the brick. We basically cuffed ourselves and signed our confessions, but we got out. And you're still pissed? We even got a car out of the deal."

Hearing this, Mase started laughing too. With the two of us laughing at him, Memo kept driving. "Man, fuck ya'll." He shook his head and smiled. "This car's a piece of shit anyway." He started laughing too now. He slammed the accelerator to the floor and turned the steering wheel. He was cutting through the sand, heading straight for the water.

"Memo?" I said.

"Hey, c'mon," Mase said. Hearing the worry in our voices, Memo laughed more.

When the car hit the water, Memo hit his head on the steering wheel. I had braced myself for the impact but still ended up kissing the dashboard. Mase braced himself too, so he came head and shoulders over the seat as gently as he could. None of us were hurt, except for a cut on Memo's head.

"You asshole," Mase said before he got out of the backseat, holding the backpack over his head. Memo had managed to get the car out to where the water was up to Mase's waist. Waves pushed water into the car's open windows, and water rose up from the holes in the floorboards. Memo and I got out of the car, getting soaked in the process. He wasn't laughing anymore, but he was still smiling.

We all waded back to shore. Mase was angry, but he had managed to keep the bag dry. I was upset too, but I couldn't be too angry with Memo. After as long as I've known him, this didn't get to me.

"You're a real genius, you know that?" Mase told Memo, who was still bleeding. Memo just looked out at the car.

"Can you believe it got out that far?" he asked. Mase and I looked out at the car.

"Damn, it is far. And it's going down fast," I said.

"You know how long it's going to take the ass of that thing to go down? You asshole." Mase looked out at the car. Its trunk and gas tank were still keeping its tail end floating above the water, but only slightly.

"Let's go," Mase said. "Can you call someone to get us?" He looked at me.

"Yeah," I said.

I was about to reach for my phone when Memo gave a shout, "Shit!" and ran out into the water toward the car.

I looked at Mase and he looked at me. We didn't know what Memo was doing. He had a hard time wading through the waves to get to the car. At this point the water was over his shoulders. He walked up the side of the car to the driver's door and dove in. He wasn't under for too long before he had to come up. "Goddamn it!" he shouted, slapping at the water in front of him, then went back down.

He was down awhile longer. He came back up and made his way to us. We could see that he was muttering angrily to himself. I was looking at his face to see what he was saying as he got closer to shore, but Mase wasn't. He saw why Memo had gone back out.

"The gun," Mase said to himself. Then he cupped his hands unnecessarily and shouted, "You dumb asshole!"

Memo picked up the gun and pointed it at Mase.

"Go ahead, shoot me with your water gun," Mase said and then laughed. He looked at me and expected me to laugh too. I kept looking at Memo coming in with the waves. I couldn't be sure, but from where I stood, I thought I could see Memo trying the trigger. I don't really think so, though.

He got back to the shore panting, and put the gun in his waistband. He stood bent over with his hands on his knees. Seeing him like this, Mase and I didn't say anything.

"You calling someone to get us?" Memo asked between deep breaths.

I nodded and pulled my phone from my pocket. I couldn't believe it when I looked at it, but, then again, it figured. "My phone isn't going to work," I said. I pressed at its buttons and put it to my ear. "It got wet. It's fucked."

Mase didn't say anything. Memo just kept sucking wind. I kept playing with my phone, hoping that randomly jabbing at its buttons would make it work.

"I saw a pay phone back that way, not too far." Memo said.

"You're crazy, you know that?" Mase said. Memo nodded his head in agreement. "We could have lost everything if I hadn't thought fast," Mase added.

"We'll talk about your cut later," I said. "My phone was brand new."

"I'll buy you a damn phone." Memo had finally gotten his breath back. "I'll have enough money to buy you five phones."

We walked toward the phone booth Memo had seen, retracing the path we'd cut to get there. Mase held the backpack, I held my broken phone, and Memo pulled his gun out and was examining the damage he'd done to it.

"You'll have enough money to buy a new gun too," I told him.

"This one was my dad's, the fucker. All I need is a cop to knock on my door because he found this gun in a piece-of-shit car in the bay," Memo said.

"Well, we still have to wait for someone to pick us up," Mase said.

"Stop complaining. We're at the beach," Memo replied.

I was cold, tired, and hungry. I knew I had more money coming to me than I'd ever seen in my life, but I didn't have it on me, and I didn't have a way to get home. I didn't want to have to deal with the added misfortune of being stuck at J. P. Luby Beach.

"You know what, Memo?" I looked out at the ugly water and wondered if any crowds would show up later in the afternoon. "Fuck the beach."

I called my cousin, for real this time. He said he's pick us up in about an hour, which meant we could be stuck there all day. We stood at the pay phone for a while, quiet.

"What about that cop?" Mase finally broke the silence.

"They were going that way," I told him, pointing to where we came from.

"Yeah, but they'll have to come back this way to get to their van or bus or whatever," he said.

We all looked at each other. I shook my head and walked away from the water. Mase and Memo followed. We climbed over and lay on the far side of the sand dune behind the phone. We lay there quietly, watching the surf pull the salty, brown-green cover off the trunk of the car we hadn't ditched well enough. The sun rose high above us in the sky, making us sweat even more than having to watch a sheriff's deputy supervise people who had gotten caught, as they cleaned the beach below us.

Lost Days

The shop was near empty when Virginia walked in. This was the benefit of taking the day off from work and going on these explorations and adventures, as she thought them to be, on a weekday. She had just gotten out of a movie at the Century multiplex. Tinseltown was closer to her house, but Bobby said he hated it, because it was too "ghetto." While just a couple of weeks ago, someone had been shot dead in the parking lot, making Virginia burn with embarrassment at Bobby being proven right, it wasn't just the multiplex (which she started calling a multiplex after his first trip home from school because "plays are produced at theaters; movies are screened at multiplexes") that Bobby thought so little of. It was all of Corpus, all of his home.

She went to the first feature of a foreign film, Chinese, she thought, but she wouldn't dare guess, because Bobby would probably correct her and tell her something about the rich cultural differences that separate the countries of Southeast Asia. She had learned about those rich cultural differences when she herself was in college, and she wondered if her forgetting them spoke to the differences in quality of education between the one she got at CCSU (which she still forgets to now call A&M CC) and the one he got at Stanford. That was probably it, she thought, but also that he was just so much smarter than her, so much more intelligent.

She wouldn't have ever gone to a foreign film before, not even one in Spanish (they were so hard to understand with their heavy Spain- and Mexico-Spanish dialects), but she was trying to understand her son and his likes—trying to get closer to him by conforming to his aesthetic sensibilities, to become someone her son would like, say, to spend an evening with, rather than someone he loves and spends time with only out of appreciative obligation.

One word she had managed to remember from college was *philistine,* and when he said it she had to leave the room so she could cry the tears she tried so often to hold back.

"I don't mean to disparage the whole of Corpus as being 'ghetto,'
because that connotes a certain socioeconomic status," he said, trying to
backpedal as delicately as he could out of a comment he'd made at the dinner table that offended Beto, her husband, his father. He had always spoken
that way; Stanford didn't do that to him. "It's just that there's a culture here
which is such that one can't be challenged or even stimulated intellectually.
There's no art, no progress toward it or high culture. It's a city of . . . of . . .
philistines."

It would have hurt less if he'd just stuck with calling the place "ghetto."
Virginia knew what she did and didn't have, and that she raised her son
where and how she and Beto could afford to. So their neighbors were a little
shady. They were still good neighbors. So their neighborhood was run-
down and their house a little small. It was still their home.

"I mean, this place doesn't even have a Starbucks," Bobby said finally,
as if the city's lack of a franchise coffee shop was all the proof his point
needed. When his father didn't change his angry expression, Bobby shook
his head, said "Sorry," and bowed his head to face the carne guisada, rice,
and beans Virginia had made special for him. Virginia excused herself from
the table and didn't leave her room until dinner was done and Bobby had
left to see some friends in town from school and some who had never left.

That was five years ago. Since then, a girl and a PhD program had
brought him back to Texas, and Virginia had been trying her best to bridge
the gap that separated them. She had made progress, but it mirrored too
closely their geographical separation. Sure, he wasn't in California anymore,
but there's not much difference between Stanford and Lubbock when your
husband doesn't fly and your son is always so busy. She read authors she
heard Bobby talk about and saw movies he said looked good during the
coming attractions at the multiplex (they caught a movie every time he
came home). She would talk to him on the phone about the books and
movies, and when he would start in on his talks of theory and subtext, she
would always fall back on the same line: "Son, I teach the third grade. I
haven't read a book without pictures or seen a movie without talking animals for as long as I can remember. At least not without you."

She had joined a book club and taken to watching movies that even
Bobby hadn't talked about. She was happy to report to him that she had
even joined the art society at the Corpus Christi Art Center ("Yes," she told
him. "We have an art center."), which held monthly wine-tasting parties.
Bobby seemed amused, if not wholly pleased, by her efforts. It was in this

spirit that she went to the multiplex that morning and walked into the newly built Starbucks, just two days after its grand opening.

A wall of coffee smell met Virginia at the store's threshold. It was thick and heavy, and it made her gag. She walked to the seat nearest her (a plush armchair), sat down, and put her head between her legs.

Why did she react that way? Why was she so affected by the smell of coffee? She liked coffee, drank it every morning. Could this all have signaled another distance separating her from modernity and from culture and from Bobby? Of course not. She hadn't been sitting for more than a couple of minutes when she got up, shook the nerves out through her arms, and laughed at her own silliness. Dr. Heckman, she supposed, had been right to prescribe her the medications when Bobby first left and she couldn't bring herself to face a day or go anywhere without having panic attacks and crying spells.

But that was so long ago. She had taken cycles of her meds, gotten better, and weaned herself from them. She could probably remember the last time she'd had an attack like this one, but she didn't want to, so she didn't try.

She walked up to the counter of the shop and was intimidated by the menu board until she heard the man in front of her order a coffee. He called it something else, but she was sure he'd ordered a plain-Jane coffee. When it came her turn to order, she said, "I'll have the same as him."

"One venti coffee, coming up," the girl behind the counter said with a smile. Virginia had taught her some years ago, but forgot her name, so didn't mention it.

Virginia prepared her coffee with half-and-half and three sugars, sat back down on the plush chair, and looked around her. It was an okay place. New. Trying to be new, hip. She took a sip of her drink and couldn't see how a place that charged this much for coffee, which she admitted right off was strong, could usher Corpus into some new stratum of relevance. Would this place raise the literacy rate? Would it lower the teen pregnancy rate? Would it make people drive better? No. It was just one more thing that could be crossed off the list of things the city didn't offer. If only a respectable bar and a decent music scene could pop up like this coffee shop did, out of nowhere in a shopping center that one always drives by but never notices until there's a banner announcing a grand-opening or going-out-of-business sale, her Bobby could come home.

She sat there allowing herself to relax, to be lulled by the heat of the coffee. She enjoyed her days off. She started taking her sick and personal days, ones allotted in a given semester, and then the back days accumulated in years of never calling in and never taking off, when the depression hit. Then they were spent in her room or in the kitchen, cooking up feasts that she and Beto couldn't possibly have finished themselves. He would reassure her, telling her how delicious the food was and that he would take the leftovers to work for lunch and to feed his crew members.

The lost days became standard operating procedure and were tolerated kindly by her principal, especially after Dr. Heckman faxed in an excuse. When the medicine started working, when Virginia got used to the change, her days off became less about crying, then less about silent meditation, then about taking advantage of the calm, uninhabited world around her. She hadn't taken a sick day in a while, but seeing that the Starbucks had opened up, she decided that she would.

Beto had been so nice about it all. Bobby's leaving had been hard on him too, but not as hard, and that hurt Virginia at first. But when she started taking her days and seeing Dr. Heckman, he was as supportive as he knew how to be.

"Quina," he told her, "they don't give you back the days you don't use when you retire."

She finished her coffee and stood from her seat, a little jittery from the caffeine. She threw her cup away and walked over to a sales display that had caught her eye. Pounds and pounds of different blends of coffee . . . bean grinders . . . coffee machines running around $300 each. She settled on buying a coffee mug. She had a thermos at home, and the mug cost $25, but it wasn't just about function. Nothing was anymore.

She picked a stainless steel one with the corporate logo emblazoned on it. She bought it from the girl, Cindy, Virginia learned from her name tag. It all came back to her.

"Cindy Diaz. You were always a good girl in my class," she said.

Cindy lit up, took the newly bought mug from the counter, and washed it out. She began to fill it with coffee.

"Mi'ja, you don't need to do that," Virginia told her.

"It's on the house, Mrs. Hernandez. We give free coffee to cops and firefighters, why not the other frontliners of civil service?"

"Spoken so well, Ms. Diaz, but I'm already shaking from the first cup." Virginia smiled.

"No problem." Cindy cleaned out the mug and filled it with steaming hot chocolate. "In appreciation of a great teacher," she said, handing Virginia the mug.

Virginia walked away, happy. Before she reached the door, Cindy Diaz spoke to her, tiptoeing over the partition that separated the preparation area from the storefront. "I'm in college," she announced, awkwardly. "I work here part-time. I graduate this May."

"I knew you'd make it, mi'jita. I'll see you next time." Virginia waved goodbye and took her phone from her purse as soon as she got in her car.

She regretted dialing Bobby's number right after she did. What if he was in class? The tone of his voice when he answered set her at ease.

"Hey, Mom," he said, sounding like he had just been laughing at something someone he was with said. "What's up?"

"You'll never guess where I am."

"If you say Lubbock, we'll grab lunch."

"Oh, I wish. No, I'm at the brand-new Starbucks in Corpus." She didn't have any real expectation of what he would say in response.

"Wow, you guys have a Starbucks. It's about time," he said.

"I know, we're always about a decade behind the rest of the world."

"Yeah," he said with a laugh. "It suits Corpus. Starbucks is the Wal-Mart of coffee shops. I bet the opening was in the news and everything."

Virginia got a familiar feeling in her stomach and the faint onset of an ache in the side of her head. "You know what?" She turned the car on. "I think it was."

"Typical." She could hear his eyes rolling. "Trick the Christians into believing they've made it. Like they're not still where they are."

"Yeah." She forced a chuckle. "Anyway, I saw a former student working there, and she's in college and she gave me free hot chocolate, so . . . I guess I just felt like hearing your voice."

"Thanks, Mom. This dissertation is killing me. Why did I pick Chaucer, Ma? Why?"

Virginia laughed because she knew she was supposed to. "You can do it, mi'jo. You're so smart. I know you can. Anyway, I better go. My break's almost over and I have to get back to school."

"All right, Mom, I'll call you and Dad tomorrow. I love you," he said and waited for her to say, "Love you too," before hanging up.

Virginia looked at the coffee mug in her cup holder and rotated it so that the Starbucks label faced away from her. Without thinking or feeling, she backed out of her parking spot and pulled away from Starbucks. She saw Cindy Diaz wave at her from the shop in the corner of her eye but couldn't wave back, because she had already pulled onto the South Padre Island Drive feeder lane. There seemed to be a lot of cars on the road for a workday. She got onto the highway and headed south. In a few miles, she could exit Ennis Joslin to drive over to the university on the island like she sometimes liked to do, to see the twenty-somethings laughing and walking and talking—matriculating. She would probably keep going south, though, and end up at the national seashore. Watching the waves lap up the litter on the beach to carry it away to far-off lands or to sink it at the bottom of the gulf always calmed her down, made her feel better, like it was she that was being whisked away, or at least crushed under tons of cold, dark, peaceful pressure.

Ridin' like a Balla

Eric devised a plan regarding the wheels he would buy for his car after great consideration. He would get the wheels from Rent A Tire, who leased their tires and wheels for the cheapest prices of all the rent-to-own tire shops in Corpus, though their interest rates were the highest. Eric knew this but was not worried. He was going to be smart about getting his wheels.

The beauty of Eric's plan was that he didn't have to get a new car. His 1998 Grand Marquis would be so fly with the rims he would get that even if he didn't paint the car glitter-flake, candy-apple red and fix its dented-in grille, as was his plan, it would still be the hottest ride on the block.

Eric would buy P7000 Pirelli Supersport tires wrapped around twenty-four-inch Conquest rims made by Mondera. When he went to Rent A Tire, the salesman tried to sell him twenty-four-inch chrome spinner rims. Eric just said, "Nah," and let out a slightly condescending chuckle. The salesman did not notice. Spinner rims were too flashy, too tacky; they were beneath him.

The salesman didn't quite understand when Eric laid out his plan. He wanted to buy two wheels. The wheels were $599 each. If someone wanted to buy a set of four, they could get it for $2,200 even, thirty days same as cash. Eric didn't have $2,200. He didn't even have $599, but he was going to get the wheels. He'd heard from a friend who got into a car crash, ruining one of his fifteen-inch gold-plated Prime 258 rims when he drove it into a curb, that single wheels, sold either as replacements or as spares, which doubled as trunk ornaments, were sold at a discount—sixty days same as cash.

So Eric bought the wheels. They came out to $600 even, each, the Pirelli tires included. He took the wheels home and, before having his cousin help him change them out with his old ones, thought long and hard about exactly where he would put them on his car. He decided to put them on the car's passenger side—one in front and one in back. It made more sense for him to put the tires in the back of the car, but this way he would look good to the pedestrians he passed on the sidewalk, and at least half of the drivers he passed would think he was a balla.

He took extra shifts at the grocery store where he worked, and that was working fine, but he realized he would need another source of income, because he couldn't pay his rent, child support, and utility bills and still have enough money left over to cover the $1,200 before the two months were over. He was working sixty-hour weeks and had forgone seeing his daughter so he could spend time at the malls and skating rink selling nickel and dime bags he got from his neighbor, who was pretty big shit, for a small-time dealer. He had come up with $550 by the end of the first month and was feeling good about his plan, when he took his first payment into Rent A Tire.

He was quite chagrined, however, when he got to the store and was informed that the store's policy had changed on replacements and spares. The wheels would still be sold at a discount, but now they were sold thirty days same as cash. The salesman also told him that at the end of the month, the replacements were going to be sold cash-only, because, as went the company's logic, if a customer could afford to have already paid off their original set of four tires, they could afford to buy a spare and buy it cash. So instead of making his first payment, he signed a lease agreement on two more tires. He would have one month to make the $1,650 he needed to buy all four tires in full, so, since he couldn't, he would aim for half and have to swallow the exorbitant interest that would accrue thereafter.

He worked sixty hours a week but hit a setback when his daughter fell ill with pneumonia. He paid the co-pay on his unemployed ex-girlfriend's government aid—it's not like he was about to let himself be a bad father. The month was winding down. The $750 he had saved was not yet enough to pay off half of the wheels before the 36 percent interest began to accrue. Two months, to the day, after walking out of Rent A Tire with a pair of wheels, his time was up. Eric got an idea. He went downtown and was given $125 for the all the sperm he could jack off into a cup after he fudged some truths and told some creative lies on an application. He needed $325 more.

When he pulled his car into the garage at his house, he saw what he would turn to for the last bit of money he needed. He put all four of the old tires from his car, stock twenty-inch ones that he knew he could sell at a used tire shop, into the trunk of his car. When he got to the shop, Banuelos Tire and Wheel, he tried to sell the tires for $45 each. He got only $35 for each—$15 per tire, $20 per wheel. This bought the grand total to $1,015. Eric was still $185 short of half. He was heartbroken. This was the last day he had before interest would start accruing on his tires. He could go into Rent A Tire the next morning and give them all of the money he had. Thirty-six percent interest on $1,385 isn't much more than 36 percent interest on $1,200. But still, Eric had wanted to be able to say he did it the smart way—that he made off like a thief. At least this way he could still make off with tires. Before he left Banuelo's, Eric was asked a question that didn't immediately register as pertinent to him.

"You know where I can get some weed?" the tire shop attendant asked.

Eric realized that he had still not sold all of the weed he had gotten from his neighbor. He had easily $60 worth of weed, but he asked for only $50. It's not like he was a drug dealer. When Eric asked why the attendant had thought to ask if Eric knew where to find weed, the attendant said plainly: "The rims. You look like a hustler."

It was late when Eric left Banuelos, too late to go to Rent A Tire, which had closed at five. He would have to wait until the next morning. He slept with the money under his pillow. The $1,065 cash felt so much lighter than the two months he'd spent saving, working, and hustling. He woke early in the morning so that he could get to Rent A Tire before it opened—responsible and smart as anyone who ever wanted to ride like a balla. When he walked out the back door, he hadn't taken even one step outside when he saw the doors to the garage open and a neon orange note taped to the windshield of his car. The color of the note told him all he needed to know about why the garage door was open and his car was on cinder blocks, barefoot and naked. He hadn't read the fine print on his rental contract that no one ever reads. He'd had thirty and sixty days, respectively, to get money into the shop. When he didn't, the account became delinquent, and, as with any rent-to-own shop in his neighborhood, Rent A Tire didn't have to call before they came to pick up their property. Eric understood. That was a smart way to run a business.

Please Don't

"Please don't leave me alone," Jonathan said. "You're all I have."

Hearing those words coming out of his mouth, Jonathan hated himself. Is there anything more pathetic than begging to be loved? Who would want to be loved out of pity, just to not be alone? Jonathan would.

Stephen rolled his eyes at this, and Jonathan grabbed him by the lapel of his black corduroy blazer. Stephen grabbed Jonathan by the wrist and, without much effort or force, made Jonathan side-scoot away an ass-length on the bench they shared, so as to not have his elbow bent back. Stephen gave Jonathan a look like you would at a dog who'd just pissed on the rug, or a kid who brought home a failing report card not for lack of effort but because he was just plain dumb.

"Don't touch me like that," he said and let go Jonathan's skinny wrist.

"I'm sorry, baby," Jonathan said. He put his palms on Stephen's face and ran his fingertips through the hair on his temples.

"Don't touch me like that, either. And don't call me baby." Stephen pulled his too-tight blazer as shut as he could get it across his muscular chest, as if he had any shame left to hide.

"I just don't think this is me," he said. "It's not who I am."

"Oh, really?" Jonathan got up from the bench and kicked an empty Coke bottle that had fallen out of an overflowing trash can nearby. He'd meant for the bottle to fly into the water, but it died midair and landed only a foot away in the large rocks that separated the bench from the bay. "Now you're second-guessing everything? Are you still afraid to tell your parents, or are you just in denial? Because you sure suck dick like a fag."

It felt good to attack, to level accusations and to play on insecurities and open wounds. But looking at Stephen, he didn't see someone who was hurt. He saw someone taking the high road, and it made him feel all the smaller and shamed him for wanting love, and for wanting to cause hurt, and for *wanting*. Stephen was there, young and athletic and beautiful as he was, condescending from perfection to break up with Jonathan, just as he had done to be with him. They'd driven out to the park and sat down on a cold, windy night so that Stephen could be rid of Jonathan.

Just over a hundred yards behind their bench was a huge series of connected wooden castles and turrets built not too long ago at Cole Park. The city of Corpus Christi called it Kids Place. It was built recently enough for Stephen to have played there as a kid, and that fact made Jonathan feel dirty. When he was a kid, the place was a couple of swing sets and three indiscernible statues of whales that had no real playground functionality.

When he was in high school, Jonathan drove a girl out here to this park. After she gave him his first hand job, he told her he might be gay.

"That's not what I mean, and you know it. I mean us, me and you. Me and anybody." There was compassion in his eyes, and it angered Jonathan to be regarded in such a way by someone just a few years out of high school.

"So that's how it is? I show you who you are, I give you some fashion tips and take you to some clubs, and you get your strength up to go out and cruise the world? I love you, and you up and leave me?" Jonathan heard his own voice cracking, so he punctuated his stance. "You fucking asshole."

"Well, I mean, yeah. That is how it is. I'm young. I'm at school and I'm meeting new people every day. And all you do is work and then hang out with me. I don't want a boyfriend, much less a husband."

Jonathan looked at the outline the wooden castles in the distance cut in the night sky, the Harbor Bridge unlit and dead behind them on the horizon. It used to have lights that ran up its supports, making it look glamorous and somewhat futuristic. Now even the streetlights on the median were rarely lit, and in daylight one could see how badly its once silver paint job was cracked and fading.

It was common knowledge in Corpus Christi, it had been covered in the local news, that Kids Place had become infested with rats feeding on food left over from picnics at the bay front park and on the woodchips meant to soften the fall of any kid playing too hard or too fast or too roughly on the park's wooden platforms. Not very many parents brought their kids to Kids Place anymore, though Jonathan hadn't heard of anything else opening up on the same scale. They seemed to all have found new places to have fun. Only older kids, teens, came to this park now, looking for mischief, and grown men looking for somewhere public to break someone's heart.

"I have a world of people to meet and things to do. As soon as I save enough money, I'm out of here." Stephen crossed his legs at the ankles, lit a cigarette, and looked out at the lights from an offshore oil rig coming in off the water. After a while, he looked up at Jonathan, who stood waiting for him to stop playing cool. He took a long drag from his cigarette and let the smoke fall from his nose.

"Listen, I'm sorry. You've been great, but I've always known who I am." With every word, smoke fell from his mouth. Jonathan loved it when Stephen did that, it made him seem so much older than he was. "You did teach me a lot, but you didn't teach me that. You just happened to be there when I let myself express it, believe it. I'm grateful you were, really grateful. But you didn't make me. And, for your information, I told my parents last night."

There it was. The boy was walking upright. He no longer had any need for a crutch. He needed no encouragement or nurturing. All he needed now from a lover was the loving, and he could find better sources of that any-where. Obsolescence did not become Jonathan, or so Jonathan thought. But that was the fate of an old queen in a dead town with a shit job and a dying mother and a sister and two nieces who wouldn't get by without his help, financial and otherwise.

If he had the whole world in front of him, he'd take it too. He remem-bered vividly being young and free at Stephen's age. He wasn't good-looking or built like Stephen, but he was free in a time of cocaine and disco and free love without all the pseudophilosophical hang-ups of the generation before his. Now he was forty-nine years old, crying in front of a man less than half his age who was all but patting his back and telling him it was all going to be okay.

"Goddamn it," he said and pointed a finger at Stephen, ready to un-leash a rant that spewed rage and bile, putting this kid in his place and show-ing him that hearts weren't to be fucked with and that even craggy old men like him weren't just there to be used and disposed of. But he couldn't. He stood pointing and would have continued to do so until the anger in him died and he just crumbled to the ground in a pile of shame and unmet ex-pectations of himself, like so much dust—the skin and dirt we shed without noticing or missing it when it's gone—there to be abandoned and blown into the bay and let out into the gulf, if the headlights of a car pulling into the parking lot hadn't shed a spotlight on him, snapping him out of his brief daze. He stomped the bench back so hard he was surprised not to have bro-ken it.

Stephen remained unfazed. He looked over at the bench where Jonathan had kicked it, then at Jonathan, as if waiting for his next move and deciding whether or not he'd have to beat up an old man that night. Jonathan looked across the parking lot at the car that had pulled in and parked over by Kids Place. It was a Camaro, well kept enough to blow up teenagers' skirts, but not old enough to look vintage. Instead it was tacky—more NASCAR parking lot than car show floor. It was a boy and a girl—really a man and a woman, but they were young enough to be his kids.

Jonathan again felt less-than. He sat down on the bench and collapsed onto Stephen, who gave him a shoulder to lean on and grabbed hold of his hand. He interlaced his fingers with Jonathan's. They'd never held hands like this, and Jonathan thought Stephen cruel for turning over another stone before walking away from everything. But, he had to admit, it felt good.

"Come on, Jonathan. Let's be grown up about this, it's not like you'll never see me again. You're probably my best friend in Corpus. And it's not like we can't get together. We just won't *be* together. I mean, seriously, Mr. Discotheque, all the stories you told me about your younger days. When did our deviant lifestyle stop being deviant?" Stephen laughed.

"When I got old," Jonathan wanted to say, but the cold air calmed him and settled him in such a way that he felt exhausted and satisfied, like a child who's cried himself to sleep.

"Let's get out of here," Stephen said. "It's freezing. I'll buy you a latte and one of those muffins you like."

Jonathan tensed his neck and shoulders when Stephen tried to get up.

"Wait just a minute," he said. "Once we leave here, it's over. We're over. Once we get in my car and pull out of this parking lot and onto Ocean Drive, we're just two people who used to love each other, or at least who used to fuck each other. Let me hang on to this for just a little longer."

Stephen laughed softly and Jonathan didn't feel the butt of a joke. He felt like Stephen understood, or was at least trying to. Stephen relaxed and looked out at the water.

"Jesus, you're so melodramatic. I swear, you'd better not stalk me or I'll file a restraining order on your ass." They laughed. "And you'll always be someone I loved. Always."

Time sort of stood still then. The world died, and the two lovers sat on the bench letting the darkness of the night around them meld with the blackness of the bay waters in front of them, setting them adrift in an ocean of beautiful desperation, disconnected from the reality that they would leave this place as friends who would eventually become strangers—a story to tell future flames and therapists. On the calm waters of denial, Jonathan could meditate on the fact of who he and Stephen were, and came to the conclusion that what would happen was for the best. But he still did not want to leave.

The sound of shouting brought them back.

Behind them, the couple who had parked their Camaro near Kids Place were arguing. She was crying. He was flailing his arms around and even giving a jump up and down for effect. She turned away from his shouts, he ran around like a small puppy or a zealous basketball defender to stay in her face.

"Well, shit, it looks like you drove us out to breakup cove or something," Stephen said.

"Yeah, I guess I did." Jonathan scooted away and stretched his legs.

"Hey, I didn't mean anything by it."

"I know, but it's time to go, and I want that latte."

Jonathan and Stephen walked arm-in-arm to the car, a small but well-kept CRX parked in the spot nearest their island bench. Jonathan pressed the button on his car alarm keychain that unlocked the doors. Stephen walked to the passenger door and had pulled it open when Jonathan stopped in front of the car. He had been looking at the ground in front of him, dizzy and light-headed from the excitement of being ready to let go, and slightly nauseated at the prospect of actually having to do so.

The slap rang loud and clear from across the parking lot, pulling Jonathan out of his head. He looked up at the girl holding her hands in front of her mouth, like she was biting her nails, in shock at what she had done to the boy, who was holding his face and cursing having been hit.

"Ha, probably serves him right," Stephen said.

Before Jonathan could look over and roll his eyes at Stephen, he saw the boy charge the girl, who reeled back, almost falling off the sidewalk. When the boy reached the girl, he met her with a fierce punch in the stomach that Jonathan could have sworn lifted her off the ground.

"Oh—" he heard Stephen begin but didn't stick around to hear the rest. He ran full tilt toward the boy and girl. The girl didn't have time to fall to the ground before the boy put his hand across her face.

"Hey," Jonathan yelled breathlessly.

The boy had pulled his leg up in preparation for stomping the girl, who was now on the ground, no longer crying for how hard she was gasping to catch her breath. He turned and saw Jonathan approaching. The sight of him must have been fierce, because the boy abandoned his anger for a second and seemed to contemplate getting in his car and driving away. As

Jonathan got closer, however, the fire seemed to overtake the boy again, and he squared up, fists at his sides, ready to fight.

Jonathan got to within ten feet of the boy and stopped. He held his hands up, palms out, to show he didn't want to fight. The boy was wearing prefaded Abercrombie pants and a navy blue fleece jacket with, of all things, a pair of brown flip-flops. He was tall and thick, not built or fat, with blond curls and blue eyes that would have driven Jonathan wild in his younger years, when self-hatred was the name of the game, and brown guys seemed too much like his cousins, like him.

"Knock it off," Jonathan said. "Get in your car and get out of here or I'll call the cops."

"Why don't you mind your own business? Leave us the fuck alone, and I won't kick your ass. Or your fucking boyfriend's ass." The boy pointed behind Jonathan's shoulder, and Jonathan heard the sound of Stephen quickly approaching.

"I mean it, just go. Right now. Get out of here and don't come back, and it'll all be done," Jonathan said.

He could feel Stephen standing behind him and was glad to have him there. He was big and strong, and Jonathan knew that his own wrinkled, bony appearance would do nothing to scare a being of juvenile rage and adolescent testosterone—not one who could do what the boy had just done to the girl, who remained on the ground in a sort of sad puddle of herself. He looked down at her, then up at the boy.

"Go," he said softly.

The boy looked at Jonathan, and at Stephen over his shoulder.

"Faggot pussy," he said. He looked at the girl on the ground, and, his lip curled in disgust, he took a hard step toward her.

Jonathan ran the ten feet between him and the girl and stood blocking her from the boy.

"I may be a faggot pussy, but if you touch her again, I will fucking kill you and not spend a second in jail for doing it."

The boy stood where he was, boiling in his skin for a moment, and then spat more wind than saliva at the girl. Jonathan balled his fists at his sides and walked a slow, calm walk at the boy, who did a sort of hop around the front of his car, got inside, and pulled out of the parking lot.

Driving away, he shouted, "Fuck you and your bitch boyfriend."

"Fuck you," Jonathan shouted back. "He's my ex-boyfriend."

"Did you call the police?" he asked over his shoulder at Stephen. When he turned to hear Stephen's answer, he saw that Stephen was crying hard and had been the whole time. Jonathan wanted, for a second, to console him, to calm him down and tell him that it was all over, but instead he went to the girl, who was still fighting for air on the ground.

"Did you?" he yelled at Stephen, who was just standing there with his hands on his head.

"No, I tried to dial while I was running, and I dropped the phone. Then it was like, do I stop and get the phone or do I go and help? So here I am. I'll go get the phone." Stephen was talking fast, blubbering between sniffles.

"Just stay here in case he comes back," Jonathan said in a firm tone that he hadn't expected to use, one that told him he was in control, that everything was okay.

"Hey, sweetie, don't worry. He's gone. You're okay now." He spoke softly to the girl, and, as slowly and gently as he could, he put his palm on her right cheek, the one that hadn't just been smashed by someone she used to love.

She seemed to snap out of a daze and kicked back a bit at the feel of Jonathan's touch.

He pulled back, telling her, "It's okay. He's gone. I'm here to help you. It's okay."

She looked around the parking lot, as if checking that he wasn't wrong or lying. Then she reached her arms out to Jonathan, who got on his knees and hugged her.

"It's okay," he kept telling her. "It's okay."

The girl didn't look too young. She was definitely older than twenty. But she was small, and her seeking comfort and shelter in his arms reminded Jonathan of his niece and of his little sister as she was years ago.

"Should I call the cops?" Stephen asked, not yet calmed down.

"No, we'll take her to the hospital." Jonathan didn't want to look at Stephen, to be disconcerted by his panicking.

"What, like walk her there?" Stephen asked. Spohn Shoreline was just across a grassy hill, on the other side of Ocean Drive going toward the Harbor Bridge.

"Really, Stephen?" Jonathan threw his keys over his shoulder at where he thought Stephen was standing. "Bring the car over here."

"You know I can't drive your car," Stephen said. "I can't drive stick."

"Take off the parking brake, put it in reverse, then in first to get over here. It's not fucking rocket science." Jonathan took care, hard as it was, not to raise his voice and startle the girl further.

"I can't," Stephen said.

"Fine. Stay here with her and I'll bring it over." Jonathan tried to pull away, but the girl would not let him. She began whimpering loudly.

"Okay," he told her. "I'm not going anywhere."

He put his right forearm under her knees and his left under her back. When he got up, Jonathan couldn't tell if the girl was light or if he was stronger than he'd thought. But after covering the distance to his car with the girl's head on his shoulder, his back was burning and his legs shaking.

Stephen opened the passenger door and tried to climb into the car, but Jonathan asked him what he thought he was doing. This stopped Stephen and allowed Jonathan to put the girl in the front seat.

"I was just getting in," Stephen said quietly.

"You can get in on my side. You see me carrying a girl across a parking lot, right?"

Stephen said, "Sorry," then walked to the driver's side door.

"No, I'm sorry. I just want to get her to the hospital," Jonathan said, then gave him a gentle slap on the back.

"Not about that," Stephen said before getting in the car. "About everything."

Then he got in. He climbed over the downfolded bucket seatback and buckled his seat belt. Jonathan realized then that he didn't need Stephen's apology for everything else. Everything else had already happened. It was over and done, and having begged and pleaded for love earlier that night could have been years ago on a tiny island adrift on the black waters of desperation.

He got in and started the car.

Backing out of the parking spot, he asked the girl, "So did you break up with him?"

"No," she said, no longer sobbing, just hunched over with her left hand on her face. "He broke up with me."

"And what?" Stephen asked from the backseat. "You just slapped him for that?"

Jonathan gave Stephen a look through the rearview mirror that silenced him.

"It's all okay," he told the girl, putting the car in gear. "We're just going right there."

Waiting for oncoming cars to pass so he could pull onto Ocean Drive, Jonathan was surprised by how well lit the street was. It was the nicest stretch of real estate in town. Local newscasters and politicians all had houses there. Selena and her husband had built a house on it before she died, and it still stood, lived in by someone else but still a sort of ghostly figure if you knew what it had been meant to be. He turned right onto the street and had to get over to the left lane immediately, as the hospital entrance was the next light up. The yellow streetlights were nothing compared to the hospital's white, green, and blue lights, shining brightly, like a lighthouse, letting people know that refuge, salvation could be found there.

Letting Go a Dream

Ana walked to the side of her son's house to take a look at his backyard before knocking on his front door to announce her presence. Marcos's backyard was big, but Ana wasn't looking at the lawn or trees. She was looking at the paved path that led to a basketball hoop behind his house. This might all work out. Her sons hadn't let her down yet. She walked to the porch and adjusted her hair in her reflection in the window of the screen door before opening it and knocking on the wooden door behind it.

She didn't bring it up during dinner, or even afterward when Regina, her daughter-in-law, was putting Israel, her grandson, to bed. She waited until everything had calmed down and it was only Marcos and her sitting in his living room on his leather sofa/love seat set, not watching the plasma TV that was tuned to Univision (a courtesy Marcos extended to his mother every Monday after their weekly dinner, and any other time she visited when his Nittany Lions weren't playing). "What's new, Mama?" he asked, like he asked every Monday. This time, there was something new.

"A constable came to my house today," Ana said, looking at the TV, trying for nonchalant.

"About Jesse?" Marcos put his Pacifico down on a coaster on the end table next to his chair, kicked his recliner closed, and sat up straight.

"No." Ana waved away Marcos's concern with the back of her hand. "Of course not. Well, I mean, if you think about it. Sort of."

"What does 'sort of' mean?"

"Well, Mrs. Jimenez from across the street has been calling in complaints to the county. At least I think it's her, entremetiche malcriada. Can you believe she's been calling complaints in for four years? And so the constable showed up today threatening to fine me if I don't get rid of your brother's car by the end of the week. And after that, I'll get fined every day, and if I don't move the car in a month, I'll get sent to jail." She picked up her café con leche, blew it a bit cooler, and sipped at it while watching

Fernando del Rincón segue from a story on border violence to one about an Argentinian starlet's recent weight gain.

"So get rid of it," Marcos said quickly. His mother gave him a look, put her drink down, and crossed her arms and shook her head. She wasn't even trying for the three-hit combo of the look, arm crossing, and head shake, which she'd perfected in forty years of motherly and spousal "I'm not angry, just disappointed"-ing. It just came out, and it worked. "All right, how much is the fine?"

"Three hundred seventy-five dollars at the end of the week. Then it's $25 a day for the first week, $35 a day for the second week, and $45 for the third week. Then it's the cuffs."

"Well, they're not messing around. So, okay, what do we do?" Marcos asked.

"We're going to have to find somewhere to put it," Ana replied, picking up her drink.

"What about Tia Loli's? She has the carport by her house that she doesn't use."

"I haven't spoken to her in close to a year. Since she didn't come to your father's funeral. I'm not going to call her."

"And how about out at the ranch? 'Buelo wouldn't mind having it out there, and there are no neighbors to call in complaints," Marcos said and got up from his chair and walked out of the room. "I'm listening," he said from the kitchen. "¿Mas café?"

"No, thank you." Ana raised her voice to be heard through the wall. "I looked into it, and it would be really expensive to have the car towed all the way to the other side of Greenton, so no. That won't work."

Marcos walked into the room with a fresh Pacifico and a mollete on a plate. "I'll tell you right now, Mama, I'll barely have enough money to cover the first fine if it takes you more than a week. The company changed health-care providers without telling us, and when Israel broke his arm, I had to pay a lot of money out of pocket that I won't get back until the new coverage kicks in. So my budget is shot for the month. What are we going to do?"

"Well, mi'jo, I was thinking we could keep the car here, in your backyard. At least until we think of what to do with it." Ana gave Marcos the sad eyes, the "you can't say no to your mama" eyes. They always worked on her husband and on Jesse, but not on Marcos.

"No. No way," he said. He was trying to be firm, but Ana wasn't fazed. It's hard to take your son's manly stand seriously when he has colored-sugar crumbs on his shirt.

"Marquitos, it's only until I can think what to do with it. And, besides, he's up for parole next month."

Marcos rolled his eyes and shook his head, his patented "whatever you say" defense—he was his mother's son.

"There's nothing else to do with it. Loli is all you have here. You can't take it to Greenton. What else is there? Me. And I can't have that thing in my backyard. Israel and his friends from the block play there all the time. It's dirty, and there are rats in it. No."

"Well then, what do I do? Pay fines I can't afford? Go to jail? Is that what you want, your mother in jail?" Ana pulled crumpled tissues out of her purse and dabbed at the tears in the corners of her eyes—her finishing move. For anything else, it would have been the nail in the coffin, but this was about Jesse.

"So get rid of it. That's all there is to it."

"You know I can't do that." Ana abandoned the tissue and let her tears fall free. "It's your brother's car. He still talks about it when I visit him. He's going to put rims on it and paint it purple and airbrush an Aztec warrior on the hood. I can't get rid of it. It's his car, his investment."

"He's got three years left. Three years. I can't have that car in my yard for three years. I'm sorry. You have to get rid of it."

"But he has a parole hearing next month," Ana whined to her son.

"Like the one he had last year and the year before that? He's not getting paroled. He is going to serve out his sentence in full, and we're going to have to keep driving five hours to Huntsville and putting money in his commissary account and praying he doesn't get killed in there and taking care of the shit he left us with. And I'm not adding a car to all of that shit. Not in my backyard where my son plays, not at my home." Marcos finished his beer, grabbed his mother's cup, and left for the kitchen.

"But he might get paroled. You don't know," Ana said when Marcos returned with a new beer and a fresh cup of café con leche that he placed on her saucer. "You don't know."

"And what tells you that they aren't going to find another weapon when they toss his cell this time? And if they don't, he's going to get into a fight before next month. You know there are people who have it in for him. Regina's cousin told us when he got out. Jesse's in deep with his crew in Huntsville. He's pissed people off, dangerous people."

"And what, that's his fault?" Ana asked.

"Listen, I love my big brother. I know he has to do what he has to do to live. But there's a reason he is where he is, and a reason he'll either serve his full term in the pinta or die there," Marcos said, drank some beer, and looked away.

"¡No me digas eso!" Ana didn't mean to be so loud. She heard Israel stir in his room. She grabbed her purse and stood to walk out. Marcos followed her to the door.

"I'm sorry. We'll figure something out. *Te promeso*," Marcos said, using his very own finishing move—the "it matters enough to plead about it en español."

"So can I leave it here? Please?" Ana said from the bottom step of Marcos's porch.

"I'm sorry. We'll have to figure something else out. I'll help you pay for it."

Ana shook her head and turned away to walk to her car.

"I love you, Mama. Call me."

"I know, mi'jito. I love you too." Ana didn't turn back when she said this, and the words might have been carried away in the wind before they got to him at the threshold of his big, beautiful home.

Ana got in her car and drove around in circles, lost and confused in the labyrinth of two-story houses and luxury cars that is the south side of Corpus Christi. When she made it out of the neighborhood to Staples Street, she thought about the fact that all of this part of town had been trees and brush, ruled by deer and javelina not too long ago, before Jesse was born. She drove up the street; getting closer to home, the houses were shabbier and the graffiti on the walls and fences was more intricate and pronounced.

She made it to her street, in her neighborhood that itself used to be the south side of town but which now, depending on whom one asks, is called either central or the west, or bad, side of Corpus Christi. She parked her car in the driveway and walked to the car on her front lawn.

Jesse, Ana's pobre Jesus, el padre santo de su vida, had bought the car, a '58 Ford Fairlane, just before he went to jail six years earlier, when Marcos was finishing his last year in college. After the alleged crime—a beautiful word, *alleged,* Ana's new favorite—Jesse never came home. She couldn't afford the bail to get him out of county or a lawyer who was even only half-shitty. So he was prosecuted, and Ana and her husband, Chuy, became the proud parents of one son at Penn State and one in the state pen.

Jesse had only been able to buy a new chain-link steering wheel and floor mats for the car in his time with it, but he had told her his plans for it—the deep purple paint, the warrior on the hood, the brilliance of turning a Fairlane, not an Impala or a Monte Carlo, into a lowrider. Ana stood next to the car and ran her hand up the driver's-side tail fin.

"Como un Mexican Batmobile," Jesse had told her.

She leaned over to look in the car and put her hand on top of it, but when she did she heard scurrying and saw movement in the dark of the car. She jumped back. Ratones, taquaches, she didn't know which it was, but she hated them both to the point that her toes curled in her shoes when she thought of them.

Having jumped a pace back from the car, she looked at it whole. It had rusted over even more in the years since Jesse had bought it as a fixer-up project. The tires had deflated and the rodents had forced their way through the already holey floorboards to make it their home. She understood why the Jimenez bitch would think it an eyesore, and knew she would have thought it herself if it were on one of her neighbors' lawns. But this was more than a car without a carburetor or inflated tires. It was so much more.

Ana walked curl-toed back up to the car, scurrying be damned, and gave the top of the car a kiss, her falling tears anointing it. Baptism or last rites, Ana didn't know which. She went inside and made a phone call before going to bed.

Ana was watching a replay of yesterday's *One Life to Live* on cable, because, though she would never tell her friends this, she preferred it and its longevity to any telenovelas, terminal and impermanent as they were, running at the time. She hadn't been able to watch it uninterrupted because of the visit she'd gotten from the constable, who was nicer than he had to be for a guy carrying a gun. It was early and she hadn't had her pills for the day. She heard the truck pull up and, despite having called for it the day before, was surprised by it. She didn't expect anyone to come so early. Don't we always think we have more time than we actually do? She got up and opened the door to see a heavyset white man who looked to be in his mid-fifties, in a T-shirt and jeans that looked freshly washed but were permanently dirty due to time spent covered in oil, sweat, and dirt. His clothes made her ache for her husband.

"Morning, ma'am. Name's Wolf. I got the message you left on the machine. This is really some car." The man had already taken the liberty of opening the driver's-side door and popping open the hood. He was standing, hands on knees, looking at what internal organs the car did and didn't have. "Such a beautiful car, damn shame it's in this state."

"Yes, it is," Ana said, staying on her porch.

"And you're looking to get rid of it?" he asked, still transfixed.

"Yes, I am. My son was going to—" She stopped herself.

"Yes, ma'am, I know what you mean. My sons were always 'going to.' But that's what we're here for, isn't it? To clean up after them."

"So, how much to tow it away?" Ana returned to the business at hand.

"Well, ma'am, any other day of the week I'd give you some kind of estimate, and we'd settle at that. But I had a good weekend, three days because I took yesterday off, and I like this car." Wolf walked up to Ana but remained at the bottom step of her front porch. "It's too beautiful a car to let it get scrapped and cubed. So I'm going to take it off of your hands and keep it for me. It'll be a lot of work, so I won't pay you for the car, but I won't charge you the tow either."

Ana hadn't imagined anyone else wanting the car. She hadn't really imagined what would happen to it, other than it being taken away. And now this Wolf character stood in his work clothes with his rested smile and offered to take it for free. Having it gone was one thing, but letting another man take it and live out her son's dream through it was something altogether different. She stood, quiet, for a moment.

"Ma'am, I'll take good care of it and have it rolling in no time. You can't put down a filly when she's got more races in her. But it's up to you." Wolf walked back to the car and looked through the window at the car's interior.

Ana thought of Jesse, of how skinny and pale he'd become in prison, of what she had heard through the chisme he'd been going through on the inside, of the parole hearing in a month, and of the toothbrush-turned-shank she could feel, in all of the distance that separated Corpus and Huntsville, that he had under his bed. She imagined the day he would return home, but even in her hopeful soul's eye, she saw that day being in years, not next month. She looked at Wolf's fascination with the car and spoke up. "All right, Mr. Wolf, it's yours."

He smiled at her and they talked about getting him the title, and he got to work getting the car on his truck. He inflated the tires with an air compressor. The front passenger tire had a pretty bad hole in it; it deflated nearly as soon as he inflated it. So he lowered the ramp in back of his rig to the ground in front of the car and hooked his chains to the car's front axles. When it was all ready to go, he inflated the stubborn tire, ran to his truck, and had the winch going before all of the air had escaped the tire. When it was all strapped down and ready for moving, Wolf walked back to the porch.

"Thank you, ma'am. I'll make sure this car has a second life. It will be better than before. I promise. It's in good hands."

Ana looked at the car on the tow truck and couldn't hold in the tears. They fell, but she wiped at them angrily.

"Thank you, Mr. Wolf." She looked at him and her tears seemed to hit him like a lowrider that never was, speeding out of her life. "I appreciate it."

"Uh, yes, ma'am. I—is there anything you'll want before I go? Anything in the car?"

"Can you give me the steering wheel?" Ana asked. "I mean, if you won't be able to get it down without it, don't worry about it."

"Of course I can, ma'am. I have tons of steering wheels at the shop." Wolf walked to his rig and hopped onto the tow platform. He opened the door and jumped back as if startled. He kicked the front seat, looked back and smiled at Ana, and took the chain-link wheel off the steering column. He closed the door and jumped off his rig. Ana walked out to the lawn to meet him halfway. He gave her the steering wheel and thanked her again. When she didn't respond, Wolf got in his truck and drove off, the car behind him, five feet off the ground, leaving Ana como un Mexican Batmobile.

She stood there on the lawn, clutching the steering wheel to her chest, and looked down at the ground where the car had been parked. Six years of darkness and cover from rain had killed the ground where the car had rested. The rectangle of dirt in her otherwise green lawn looked as dead as Ana felt inside. It'd be hard for anyone passing by to not notice it. She walked forward, standing in the center of the car outline, and was disappointed with herself for not having suggested that Wolf paint the car purple. For a second she thought to call him and tell him about her Jesusito's plans but realized how pointless it would be. What fifty-year-old white guy would want an Aztec painted on the hood of his car? It was just silly, hopeful nonsense. She let it die. She would call Marcos and let him know that the situation was taken care of. Maybe she'd even ask him if they could take a drive up to Huntsville to visit Jesse and give him the bad news in person. But she could do that later. Right now, she'd sit and watch her stories.

Last Primer

John David Gomez sits waiting for me in his 1986 LTD Crown Victoria, the same one his mother used to drive, though he has touched up the car's paint and tinted its windows in the many years since she left him and the car at her mother's house so that she could pursue a future with an amateur boxer she'd known for only two days. He's parked at the end of my block, and I jog-step to his car so we can drive off before anyone sees us, though I don't know that any of my neighbors would be up at this hour. The sight of him behind the wheel of that car reminds me of his mother and those rare times when she was waiting for him after school, times when I would have to kick JD and his friends out of my classroom so I could go home to my wife and daughter. He's even smoking like she always was when she waited, though he's smoking a Black & Mild rather than the Doral 100s she used to smoke, the kind my mother had switched to toward the end of her life. I get in the car, and JD turns down the radio to greet me.

"Hey, sir," JD says as he turns the car on and puts it into gear, "you don't mind the smoke, do you?" He is wearing his work clothes. He must have just gotten off. I don't think he would go in after what we're about to do.

"JD, it's been ten years since I was your teacher. You can call me Steve." Neither of us speaks, and for a while the thumps of the wheels passing over the freeway section splits mark time. JD turns the radio back up. "I don't mind the smoke," I tell him. "My wife doesn't know I'm out, and if she wakes up when I get home, I'll tell her I went to a bar."

"How's she doing with everything?" He doesn't look over at me.

"I don't know. She was so strong after it happened. She stayed day and night with Sara in the hospital. But now that Sara's home and, for the most part, physically better, it's really hit Imelda. She sleeps a lot. So does Sara. She's taken to sharing Sara's pain pills. So, I just don't know."

It's strange being this honest with someone who sat in my classroom before his voice changed. I look at JD driving: his cigarillo, the speedometer, and the radio the only lights in the car. It's just so unreal—looking at him from the passenger seat, sitting in a car that I've never sat in but seen so many times. I feel as small as he must have felt all those times I drove him home after school, those numerous times when his mother was elsewhere after Lexington Middle School closed down for the day.

"And you?" JD looks at me.

Now I need to lie. "I'm fine. I think it hurts less, but with this investigation bullshit I'm so angry all the time."

"Yeah. I would be too." JD shakes his head. "There's a flask in the glove box. You can smell like that bar your wife thinks you're going to. Or, you know, just numb it all a bit."

I open the glove box and sitting on the flask of Tanqueray is a .38 revolver. The light of the moon shining through the window reflects blue off the gun's nickel plating. I push off the gun with the back of my hand and reach for the flask.

The mouthful of gin I throw back is burning in my belly when I pull the gun out of the glove box. "Is this the one I'm going to use?"

He glances over briefly and then looks back to the road in front of us.

"Yeah. It's a .38 like you asked for, like the one that he—" JD stops short of saying it, but the idea pronounces itself.

The gun he shot your daughter with. The pain of it all mixes with the gin in my stomach. My daughter—raped and beaten, shot and left for dead—and my near-catatonic wife are riding in the car with us now. I drink more gin, put the flask and gun back in the glove box, and try to make out stars over streetlights in the night sky.

"It's going to be fine, sir. I mean, Mr. Rodriguez. We'll do this thing now, and you can go back home knowing I'll take care of everything that needs taking care of."

Looking at JD in the dark, I can barely make out the traces of the "ABC" tattoo on his neck. I was so mad, so disappointed, when I saw him just a year out of middle school with the gang marking on his neck. The audacity it took for him to visit me at school for the first time with that ink on his neck shook me. I initially thought he was parading in, in a defiant show of freedom, telling me that he didn't need me or my respect. But when he kept coming back, after dropping out at sixteen, after getting out of prison at nineteen, to tell me he was going to be a father at twenty, I realized he was seeking proof of my respect and love unconditional. The tattoo is fading. He has others, the names of his son and wife on his forearms and the Virgen de Guadalupe on his right bicep, but now I have to squint hard to make out that first one.

"Thank you for doing this for me. This has been killing me, and I need to know I can make things right, as right as they'll get. Like I'm not just watching someone get away with doing this to my daughter. Like I can protect my family."

"I think I know what you mean."

"Thinking of how to do this, all I could come up with was you. I couldn't do this by myself. I wouldn't know how." I look over at JD, thankful, rationalizing.

"Me either." I know he's telling the truth. "But thank God for family and long-lost friends."

I drink a little more gin. What I am about to do and what's happened and the fact that I'm in this car right now are making me light-headed. I try to think of my family as we were before, and it gives me clarity. It heats my blood, and I focus on what's about to happen. We've gotten onto the interstate and are heading north. The city is almost entirely behind us. I can't stand the wait. I want this now. But we drive on. I close my eyes, lean back in my seat, and remember Sara's high school graduation. She was so confident, so strong. I can't reconcile that image of her with how she is now. All of my anger is in the gap that exists between these two versions of my daughter. I try to center myself in that anger.

"We're here," JD tells me and gets the gun out before we get out of the car. He's driven us out past the refineries, to where there are scattered bay inlets that some people try to fish if they have four-wheel drives to get them the few hundred yards into the swampy grass that leads to the water. We're parked behind two waiting cars on the side of a caliche road. Four men get out of each car, one of them an old Lumina and one a newer Pontiac. It's hard for me to see JD in the dark of where bad things happen, but I think I recognize all of the men, most of them in their mid-twenties, a couple in their late teens. They're either former students of mine or siblings of former students of mine; all of them are from the neighborhood. They all wear red, black, and white, ABC colors—that I can see. They each nod at me from in front of our caravan, and I nod back.

One of them comes over to JD and me. It's Carlos, JD's cousin, whom I taught a year earlier than JD but never thought I could save like I did JD. Carlos was too far gone; he was jumped into the gang before I even met him. I remember seeing him as my competition for JD. I pulled toward school and Carlos pulled toward ABC. Carlos and ABC won, but I stood my ground and kept JD in school and out of the gang for three years.

"Hi, sir." Carlos looks down solemnly and reaches his hand out for me to shake. I do. "How you doing?"

"All right," I say. "I'm just ready to do this thing."

Carlos smiles. "Yeah, sir. We're gonna make things right tonight. Like Hammurabus," he looks at me, eager. "I bet you thought I forgot about that shit, didn't you? But you were a good teacher. You taught a little cholo like me things like Hammurabus and his code of revenge." The one thing he remembers me teaching him, he remembers wrong. "We're gonna fuck this guy up. I mean, you even got an OG like my cousin to come out of retirement for a night. He ain't been around me and my boys since he became a daddy. But he knows who to call if he needs something. Ain't that right?" Carlos puts his arm around his cousin's neck, and I wish I had brought the gin with me. When JD remains silent, Carlos realizes his enthusiasm has violated the mood of the night. He puts his arm on my shoulder and looks me in the eyes. "I'm so sorry about what happened. We're gonna make it right. Hammurabus-style."

He walks toward the huddle of ABCers two car lengths ahead of me, and JD follows him, telling me that he'll be back. He just needs to check if everything's going according to plan. I sit on the still-warm hood of his car and am alone and scared, for the first time fully realizing that I'm here, about to do what I'm about to do.

Lack of evidence. I mean, how much evidence could a cop need? He'd done it before. They tell me he has never been this violent before—abducting and beating my Sara bloody, shooting her in the chest before running away. "That's not how this one rapes." It's been running around in my head nonstop, consuming me. "I know he did it," the detective told me. "Give me time to make it stick." He had his time. There were surgeries and hospital stays, and now there are scars and painkillers and tranquilizers and nightmares, and Abram Loredo is still free.

I look up when I hear laughter from the guys JD is talking to. He raises his voice: "This is serious." The crowd quiets down. They continue talking in near whispers. This is serious. I stand up and walk across the road, the caliche I'm walking on crunching under my feet. I walk into the waist-high grass and look out to where I know there is water that I can't see for the night. I breathe in a mixture of oil refinery burnoff and stagnant water. The stink makes me wish for home and my side of the bed and my hurting Imelda to hold.

The sound of a car nears. I turn around and see a pair of headlights coming from the direction of the highway. A cold rush turns my stomach, and I am unsure of what's happening. Before I have time to panic, JD comes over to me. "It's them." As the headlights make their way toward us, JD grabs my right hand and wraps my fist with three red-and-white bandannas. He tapes it up, balls it tight and slaps at it hard. He does the same with my left hand.

An old pickup truck parks in front of all the other cars, where the ABCers stand waiting. I walk up to join them and see two men, each in their forties, both wearing black T-shirts and black pants, get out of the truck. The driver's head is shaved, revealing tattoos all over his skull, going down to his neck, which is also completely covered in ink. The other man is wearing a gorra that covers his ears and his hair to the back of his neck. All the skin I can see on him is above his full beard and below his sunglasses. He walks around the truck and stands by the driver's-side door as the driver talks to Carlos.

They shake hands and share a hug. The driver whispers to Carlos, and Carlos gestures over to me. The driver looks at me and greets me with a high nod. JD, who is standing next to me, leans in close. "These guys are pros. Carlos knows them from when he was locked up at Huntsville. They're connected deep in the syndicate."

After a bit more talking with the driver, Carlos announces, "All right, let's do this, then."

The bearded man in the knit hat opens the door to the pickup, a two-door, and folds down the seat. "Get out," he says sounding bored. I hear gagged pleas coming from the backseat of the cab, and the bearded man says, "Don't start that again, okay. Get out of the truck right now." He pulls a gun out and sticks it into the cab. For a moment, I see Loredo's head poke out, but he falls back down onto the truck's backseat. Sighing, the bearded man reaches in with one hand and pulls out Loredo, mouth taped and hands bound behind him.

Loredo falls out of the truck and lands on his face and shoulders. The ABCers laugh and Carlos says, "Aww yeah, motherfucker. You're gonna get yours real good." Two of the ABCers stand Loredo up. Blood traces the side of his face from where his forehead hit a rock in the road. Looking at him, I can tell he's been crying. He tries to yell, so Carlos steps up to him and grabs his throat. He squeezes and after a while Loredo is shaking his head and kicking his feet. I step forward from my position in the back of the crowd.

For the first time I realize that JD's hand is on my shoulder. I look at him, and he looks at me, waiting.

I push my way through the white and red shirts, and Carlos lets go of Loredo's neck when he sees me next to him. Carlos is breathing heavily, almost panting, and there is something in his eyes that is more excitement than anger. He takes a step back, and I touch Loredo's face. He stops resisting long enough to look at me and realize who I am. When he does, he calms down, no longer kicking or trying to shout. He wipes his face on his shoulders and stares right at me.

I take the duct tape off his face and tell the bearded man, "His hands." The bearded man cuts the zip-tie that binds Loredo's hands. Loredo grabs at his wrists, sore and bloody from having fought to get free. He never takes his eyes off me.

"Why?" I say, staring hard. My fists, like every muscle in my body, are clenched, shaking at my side.

"They'll know it was you. You're the first person they'll look for," Loredo says.

I don't know if it's that he's trying to reason with me or just hearing the voice I've heard so many times denying, lying, but I swing an angry fist at Loredo, hitting him on the shoulder. Though the force of it knocks him down, the blow was unsatisfying, embarrassing even. I haven't hit someone since my childhood. Despite my having missed my mark, my audience cheers. The ABCers flanking his sides prop up Loredo, and he rubs his shoulder where I hit him.

"You think I'm worried about getting caught?" I shout. Loredo is a small man wearing a western-style shirt, jeans, and cowboy boots. They must have gotten him coming home from the cantina.

"Don't you watch the news?" Carlos interrupts me. "He's a 'beloved member of the community.' Don't you think they'll know that there're cholos who belove him?" He points at me and sniggers.

Loredo looks down, shaking his head slowly. "Look at me," I tell him. "Why?"

"I didn't do anything," Loredo whines at me.

I punch him in the face, and before he can fall to the ground, I grab him and hit him twice in the stomach. More cheers. "That's right . . . Fuck him up . . . Kick his ass . . ."

Once again, Loredo is picked up after I let him fall. His face is red where I punched him, and he is hunched over in pain, coughing.

"We're not in court. There are no recorders. You're not being interrogated." I am trying to be calm, but there is bile in my throat, and my words come out as a growl. I feel my own spittle fall on my chin. "You're going to die tonight, but first tell me why."

"I—" he shakes his head and I pull back my fist, the bandanna covering it bloodied. Before I swing, Loredo stops me. "Man, I'm sick." The pathetic truth of it shakes me, so I grab his shirt and put a forehand slap across his face. He grunts and lets out a sob. "I'm sick. That's all there is. You think I don't want to be right? Ask these thugs what they did to me, what they do to people like me in the pinta. I have parents and grandparents, and they taught me right. I just can't help it."

"So you sneak up on my girl and hit her in the back of the head, you put her in your car and drive her to an old park, you violate her," I shout, and grab his hair to pull him closer to me, "and you shoot her because you're sick? Do I have that right?"

"I don't—you don't want to talk about this. This isn't right." He winces in pain.

"You don't say what's right," I say, finally calm. "I asked why and you told me. You're sick." He looks down, beginning to shake his head again. I punch him in the head, and he is held up from falling down. I start swinging wildly at his stomach and chest and at the side of his head. With every connecting blow, there is a kinetic release of hurt and angry sadness. When I'm almost all out of my own, I pound out some for my wife and, of course, for our Sara. He becomes dead weight and the ABCers at his side let him fall to the ground. He folds into himself, arms covering his beaten body and face. I kick at his stomach once, twice, three times.

"Don't," Loredo coughs out in pain. "Please don't." He is holding his stomach, crying now. "Please don't."

"Did she say please?" I ask and stomp the heel of my shoe into his face. His nose seems to break, because blood gushes out of it onto his face and chest. He rolls on his side and covers his face, not for protection but to burrow into a shell of pain and cry. He cries full and hard, moaning in pain, sobbing deep and loud. I finally see a man in front of me, crying, probably praying for forgiveness. He's no longer a monster and, seeing the mess of blood and tears, I am satisfied, hunched over, sucking bitter air, but I stand tall—righteous and triumphant in a way that only a man having beaten to a pulp the source of all of his family's pain can be. Behind me, I hear a groan of empathetic disapproval above the shouts of encouragement.

"JD!" I call above the shouts of the crowd. He comes to my side, but I don't take my eyes off of Loredo crying on the ground.

"Yeah," he says.

"Give it to me," I tell him. "Give me the gun."

"Listen," JD starts quietly and calmly. I can hardly hear him over the shouts and excitement from the guys behind me. "You don't have to. I think you should slow down and think, because we can—"

"Give me the gun," I say again. Every second I stare at Loredo on the ground my blood gets hotter. I breathe hard and angry. Next to me, I hear JD recede. He's stepped back and I turn around to face him. "Give me the gun," I say, anxious, wanting to keep my anger focused on Loredo.

"You messed him up already. You don't need to do anything else." JD looks at me.

"Give me the goddamn gun." I have raised my voice to a shout. I am ready to strike JD or anyone who gets in the way of what I'm here to do.

JD puts his hands on my shoulders and pulls me close to him. "Sir," he says, "please don't."

I can see that JD is scared. He looks at me and shakes his head no. I am about to protest when he stops me with his eyes and tells me, "Just don't." The concentrated focus of my anger has been broken, and I look around. The shouts I have been tuning out are there to be heard, and the audience surrounding me looks on, wanting blood. Carlos is jumping around, filled with blood-fueled excitement. "What are you doing? Let him do it," he shouts at his cousin. The other ABCers shout in agreement. Their excited movement disorients me. I can see an animal bloodlust shine off of them in the light of the moon. I am dizzy, nauseated, and confused.

"No," JD tells me, and then looks back at the crowd he is no longer a part of and shouts, "No!" They quiet down and I put my face in my hands and stand thinking, my head shaking in my covered palms. All that can be heard on this caliche road at the foot of a field at the mouth of the Nueces Bay are the loud sobs and deep, wheezing breaths of Abram Loredo bleeding on the ground behind me.

In the silence I wait, centering myself in the moment. I take my hands off my face and look at JD. "Give me the gun," I tell him, pleading.

He looks at me and nods. He reaches into his pocket and gives me the gun. He places the gun barrel-first, cold and metal, wholly inhuman, into my hand. "All right," he says and I turn around. JD leans forward and speaks into the back of my head.

"Look what you've already done. You don't need to finish this."

I look at Loredo there on the ground and don't even have it in me to raise the gun. A fire in me has died, and I just can't. I hate myself for it, but I can't. I get close to the crying man and crouch down at his side. "Well then, why did it have to be my daughter?" I stay at his side for as long as it takes for him to realize I'm not going to hit him. He uncovers his bloody face and looks at me.

"At least you can have this," he tells me between sobs. I look at him and take in the sight of his face—swelling in both cheeks and eyes, blood coming from the gash on his head, the cuts above his eyes, and of course from his broken nose. I relish the sight of Abram Loredo in this state and stare until I know it's burned into my memory forever.

I stand up and Abram Loredo, ready to die, covers his face and waits to be delivered by a bullet. Behind me I hear the crowd start up again. They shuffle nervously and whisper to each other in excitement. I hand JD the gun and walk through the disappointed but understanding faces of ten criminals. They are silent and every one of them avoids my eyes as I do theirs. I get into the Crown Victoria and start in on the gin in the glove box.

After a while, JD gets in the car. He turns on the car, lights a Black & Mild, and drives us back toward civilization.

We pass under the lights of the freeway on our way to my house, and JD speaks up. "They're going to take care of it. He's going to disappear. The cops are going to come ask you questions, but we'll make sure it looks like a gang hit. They'll clean everything up and make him disappear. And he's going to hurt a lot more before it's done." I sit looking out the window, and JD smokes his cigarillo.

It's a hot night, and I'm sweaty from the beating. I wipe my brow and the duct tape on my hands startles my face with its unfamiliarity. I look down at the makeshift gloves I've forgotten I had on. They are both covered in blood, more than I've ever seen. There are spatters of blood on my face and pants. Suddenly aware that I am incriminated, stained, I claw furiously to get the bandannas off my hands. My knuckles are tender. I stare at my hands. Naked, innocuous, with grey hairs grown on them, these hands aren't meant for punching, for smashing, for punishing.

"JD, that wasn't me out there," I say, getting the last of the tape off my second hand. "I mean, thank you . . . I . . . just . . . thank you."

"I had to, sir. You've always been there for me. Even when I started messing up, you were there for me. I mean, you're one of the main reasons I left the gang." He looks over at me and then back at the road. "I knew I was going to be a dad, and you always told me I could do it, just like that. So I did. And you've done everything for me. Remember when you gave me that jacket that winter I was in the eighth grade because my grandma didn't have any money to buy me one? It was the coldest winter Corpus had seen since

'83. Any way you could help, not just me, but any student, you always did. This happened. You called me for help. I knew I had my cousin and ABC, and I knew I could help you. I knew we could give something back. I understand why you called me, and I'm honored." He looks over at me again and sees me looking down at the blood on my clothes, "There are clothes in the backseat. Change now and I'll get rid of yours."

I grab the clothes from the back of the car and start changing. "But that's not me, JD. And it's not you anymore," I tell him as I button up the shirt he has for me.

"Yes it is, sir. It's you and it's me and it's everyone. If anyone hurt my boy . . ." JD stops and takes a drag of his smoke. "And you would help me out like I helped you out. I mean, not the same way, but you would help me, like you always have."

I am quiet for what's left of the drive to my home. JD turns the car onto McArdle, and we drive past Archer, Blundell, Cheryl, Dodd, Easter, and Franklin streets until we come to Gabriel, my street—my piece of the ABC streets. As earlier, JD parks up the block from my house. He turns the car off, and we sit together for a moment. He lights another smoke, and I sit quietly, trying to regain perspective after a night of chaos, not ready to go home with blood on my hands.

After a while, JD ashes his cigarillo and looks at me. "All right, sir, I have to get going. I have to be at work by five."

Surprised by the broken silence, I rub my eyes and sit up. "Why didn't you let me do it? You brought the gun. You took me out there. Why didn't you let me finish it?"

"You're not a killer, sir. Of all the things I did back in the day, with all the dirt on my hands, I never killed anyone. I don't think I could look myself in the mirror. You need to be able to, so you can be strong, so you can teach."

"Listen, JD, I needed this. My wife needed this. I can't tell you how much I needed this."

JD waves off my thanks. "It's done. Go be a father and a husband and a teacher. Go teach kids about Hammurabi and Aristotle and all that."

I have to smile as I get out of the car. Before I close the car door, I poke my head in the car and say, "Please, JD, next time we see each other, call me Steve."

"All right," he tells me, "and you call me John. No one's called me JD since middle school."

I agree and close the door. JD drives off and I am a block from home. I stand there on the sidewalk preparing to walk back into my home that has been disturbed by so much hurt and pain. Having beaten Abram Loredo near to death hasn't changed that. I stand there readying myself emotionally for what home has become, for walking into that and going to sleep in it and waking up and cooking breakfast in it and drying my daughter's tears in it and drying my wife's tears and hiding my tears in it. I just need a minute to get ready for what that does to me. It's a hot night and my back is sweaty and I'm tired. I just need a minute.

Pawelekville

Night had fallen on Karnes County without Andy in Pawelekville, staking out the Carpentier house from the abandoned garage across Highway 123, as had been his plan. He was holed up at the Dairy Queen in Stockdale, regretting having eaten when he did, wondering if it was food poisoning, cheap beer, or nerves that had him stinking up the dirty bathroom in a hallway behind the packed dining room. The delay his guts were putting on his evening wouldn't stop him. He would proceed as planned, driving the eleven miles that separated him from Pawelekville and solving the riddle his mind had made of the house on the west side of the quarter mile of road that was considered a town.

He had stopped over in a Seguin (or would it be considered Stockdale?) eatery. It was one that he had passed many times on his way home over the last eight years but never set foot in for its so belonging to the place, to the places, to the stretch of highway between two towns where he didn't belong. He had eaten a pulled pork sandwich, assuming it to be the roadhouse's specialty, as there was a painting of a pig in a chef's hat on the wall that faced the road. He'd drunk three cans of Pearl, not necessarily trying to fit in with the locals who stared him down when he walked in but were, for the most part, minding their business, but drinking it to fit the picture in his mind of what one did in a place like that. Six miles up the road, it all caught up with him.

Arriving in Pawelekville, Andy turned left onto FM 887. His plans were further thwarted when he found the garage across the road to be not only inhabited but impassable at the sides to his car. He had planned to park his car behind the structure he thought to be empty. To stay in front of the garage he would have to park in plain sight of the highway and the Carpentier house and everyone else in town. He had not planned on needing a place to hide his car. He simply thought he would park it across the street so as not to arouse suspicion in whoever may be at the house when he arrived. But now, with the darkness of night all around him so very harshly cutting an outline of him in the nothing, the stupidity of his plan stood out like the white shirt on his back—most visible in the scant light afforded by the moon and stars, but covering up something bigger, covering Andy and covering the fact that he was probably going crazy.

He turned his car onto 887, driving along the shoulder without his foot on the accelerator, feeling out the road for a spot far enough from the main highway to be hidden but close enough so that if he had to make a quick getaway, the distance wouldn't slow him down too much. He got to a point where he could no longer hear the sounds of cars passing on 123 but could see their lights streaking by, made a U-turn, and parked in the ditch that separated the road from a tract of land shorn bald by tractor of its cotton high-top.

Walking toward the main highway and the house beyond it, Andy was glad his roadside culinary detour had emptied his bowels. He was so nervous, shaking in the back and shoulders and sweating all over, that he would have had to give up his position and all of the momentum at his back to return to the car and drive up to the nearest gas station in Karnes City, and if he'd made it there, he might just have pressed on down to Corpus Christi, that city he awkwardly called home out of obligation to the past. He pushed on, thanking the pulled pork for the detox and the Pearls for dulling his sense of reason, or at least for giving him an excuse for not heeding it.

Standing at the intersection of the two roads, Andy saw the distant, growing glow of a car's headlights approaching from the north. Here, instincts took over. He dove down on the ground and buried his face in the grass. When the car had passed, Andy got up and brushed burrs and thorns from his shirt and slacks. Peeling them from his bare forearms, he resigned himself to the fact that he was indeed crazy to be where he was. He looked out toward where he had parked his car and couldn't see it. He told himself this was a good thing. It wouldn't be seen from the main highway; he wouldn't be so greatly tempted to run back and get in and drive away from his personal crisis and southward to the bigger, realer one that awaited him in Corpus.

Andy stood on the front lawn of the Carpentier house. Really, it was the front of the Carpentier plot, as there were no bordering neighbors on the sides of their home or land. Though the moon gave little light, what it did give cast a shadow of Andy that was big and deformed by its edges slipping into the darkness around it. The sight of himself, his impression on the Carpentiers' land, breaking the stillness of night made him run—scamper, really, head and shoulders hunched to the ground, like some rodent fleeing the sound of footsteps.

He ran directly to the window that, if he had to run down the math of why he was running, *lurking,* in the middle of the night in the middle of a town only noticed for the change in speed limit on the way to and from better places, was the reason for his stop in Pawelekville. Driving home to Corpus, from home in Austin, he noticed the house, the window. The window was big, maybe seven feet tall, five across, with two-foot-wide panels on either side, making of the living room beyond it a diorama of domestic, rural, American home life. On those trips down to Corpus—always at night, always on Sundays, as he would delay his departure from Austin, from his house, his bed, his wife as long as he could—he always slowed his car to slower than the posted fifty-five through town in an attempt to take in as much of the house as they were offering that night.

Some nights, the curtain that separated what he could determine to be the living room proper from what he supposed was a sun room was closed. Most nights, the curtain was left open and Andy could see the living room lit by lamps and/or the family television. Andy counted himself especially lucky when he saw the lady of the house, a woman his passing-by glances told him was probably beautiful, definitely blond. But it wasn't the sight of the woman that had piqued his interest all those times; it was the fact of someone living.

He had imagined so many realities for the Carpentier family. They had children, at least one of high school age. On their front lawn sat a wooden cutout of a football helmet with the number forty-two on it. Aside from their son, the defensive back, Andy imagined the Carpentiers to have two younger children, as he had seen on many drives up to Austin, always during the day, right after work on Fridays, a bicycle on the front lawn of the house he could almost not recognize without light from the window inviting his eyes in for a break from middle-of-nowhere dark.

Having made his dash for the window, Andy stood there looking into the sunroom. He touched the window pane. It was plastic, hard and thick. He ran his hand down the side of the cold aluminum frame. The feel of the window, of the house, made his night real. He had to get out of the front yard. He had to get inside.

He tried the front door (above it was the sign that read "Carpentier House"), but it was locked. Don't they always say that people who live out in places like this leave their doors unlocked in case neighbors need to borrow something? Wasn't this still Texas, the most Texas of places? He walked along the side of the house, to the back, where he found the back door unlocked. Illusions and clichés validated, Andy entered the house with confidence. He was just a neighbor, a stranded motorist, maybe. He just needed help.

The back door opened into a dining room. There was a table with six chairs at it. The room was not messy or dirty, but lived-in. There was a backpack on the floor and what looked like homework on the table. One of the chairs had a shirt pulled across its back. Drying?

On the other side of a sink and cabinets overhead was the kitchen. There were Pepsis and Miller Lites in the fridge, along with leftovers and sandwich accoutrements. It looked as unorganized as one would expect it to. It fed a family. Out a swinging door from the kitchen was a formal dining room. The table was sleek, modern-looking, black or dark brown. There was a hutch with a vase and a silver tea set on it.

Across the hall from the formal dining room was the living room, bigger and less cluttered than it appeared from the road. The hallway stretched from the front door to the back of the house, where Andy logically placed the bedrooms. He walked into the living room. A sectional sofa set, L-shaped in front of a large TV. On either side of the TV were two bookshelves loaded with books of all colors and sizes, some standing upright and some lying in neat stacks.

What did people like this read? People out here? People with families? Andy couldn't make out any of the titles on the books' spines in the unlit living room. He reached for one to pull off and examine, but light from a pair of headlights out on the highway ran across the wall in front of him. Andy dropped to the ground as if the light were some kind of laser, apt to cut him across the waist and leave him to be found in pathetic, embarrassing halves on the floor of the Carpentier living room.

Out of either fear or a desire to not be existing where he was just then, Andy shut his eyes and tensed his face into an ear-ringingly tight vise, so that all he could hear was the sound of muscles tightening and his heart pounding in his chest. When he calmed down and opened his eyes to face the world he had stolen into, Andy couldn't tell how long he had hidden within himself. It could have been a few seconds or a few minutes. However long it had been, when he snapped out of his panic, he felt the need to move, to shake himself off a bit of the ground with which he'd just gotten too familiar. He pushed himself up onto his knees and crawled over to the sunroom quickly enough to get rug burns on his hands.

There was a crack in the curtain just big enough for Andy to fit his head into. He poked his head through and draped the curtains around the rest of his body. If anyone else drove by just then, they might notice a dis-embodied head, sweaty at the hairline, pale in the cheeks, and a little blood-shot in the eyes, in the big windows Andy had looked into so many times. More likely, though, they wouldn't notice anything, and this calmed Andy a bit.

He scanned the dark, empty highway in front of the house. Not a car to be seen, or any other sign of life for that matter. Looking out of the win-dow, Andy could not tell where the Carpentier land or the highway or the land behind it was. He felt like a pilot mistaking the ocean for the sky. He felt like he was falling. But then he looked up, just beyond the farthest push of horizon in front of him, and was compelled to get up off of his knees and walk full-on into the sunroom. The stars in the sky were so vivid, so alive in their deadness, so up-close-and-personal, like a nursery full of infants on the antiseptic side of a hospital window. Andy wanted to reach up and grab one, to take it home and raise it as his own little ball of burning gas and carbon. He wanted at least to touch one, to touch something, to feel it. He had walked up to the window. His nose was almost pressed up against it, he was that close. He picked his hand up from his side and was about to lay his palm on the glass that separated him from the cosmos, but his moment with the galaxy was interrupted in a manner that could only be considered rude if Andy had not been standing in someone else's sunroom, in someone else's house, trying on their life and their view of the universe.

Whether it is sensory knowledge gained from generations of on-screen pop culture—westerns, gangster flicks, cop flicks, black comedies, or prewar racist, un-PC cartoons about hunting ducks and/or rabbits—or something more innate, the sound of the hammer on a firearm being cocked back will almost always send shivers down the spine of whoever is standing at the business end of a barrel. Instead of pressing his right hand up against the window in front of him like he had wanted, Andy raised up his left to join on the other side of his chest. Standing there, open palms touching the sky by his shoulders, Andy thought of how nice it would be to meet his end there under the stars.

"You got the hands part right, and so you're still alive. But make one wrong move and I will put a hole the size of a cantaloupe in your chest," said a voice, deep and raspy, like Tom Waits with a southern accent.

The man spoke slowly, and Andy figured that this boded well for his odds of surviving the night. But what a thing to die there, like the captain of a starship that had been boarded by belligerent alien forces. Andy had half a mind to spin around and lunge at the gunman. But he couldn't. Andy didn't do things like that: lunge, engage in combat, spin around without falling over. This was probably fair. If Andy couldn't live like a starship captain, he didn't deserve to die like one. Besides, it would be rude to attack physically the man whose home he had already so rudely invaded. So he stood, awaiting instructions.

A push of cold steel on the back of his head almost knocked Andy over. It was the barrel of what he figured had to be a pretty big gun. A hand grabbed his shoulder to steady him.

"You're doing all right on your feet. Don't go falling to the ground and startling me into shooting you dead," the voice said.

Andy felt the hand drop from his shoulder to his waist. It rubbed the sides of his legs and once around the back. There was the awkward feeling of a man's hand tracing the front of Andy's pants, which was made worse for the man keeping his other hand on what Andy figured to be a shotgun as he was almost forced to bend over by the barrel while the man tried to wrap one hand around his waist while keeping the other on the trigger. The man then felt the insides and outsides of Andy's ankles. Seeming satisfied with his patdown, the man took a few steps back.

"All right, then. You can go ahead and turn around if you like."

Andy stood still, not wanting to give his back to the stars and not wanting to face what he had done that night.

"Turn. The fuck. Around," the man said, still calm.

Andy turned his body clockwise to face the man behind him. The man was holding a shotgun, a beautiful thing, really—a long double barrel leading to a single lever, elegantly and ergonomically curved, like a single stem on a pair of cherries, pulled back and ready to spring forward to strike an explosion. He was younger than his voice made him seem, probably in his forties. He was skinny, not very tall. Andy thought he was the kind of hard that bull riders were.

"Can I put my hands down?" Andy said.

"Do whatever you want with your hands," the man said, his voice still belying the sight of him, "but I'm gonna keep this here shotgun pointed at you."

Andy stood stone still, trying to figure out what he should do from what the man in front of him was saying and not. The man looked at Andy's hands and gave a small nod. Andy dropped them to his sides and dried his palms on his slacks. The man looked at him hard, trying to take in who and what had broken into his home.

"So are you some kind of salesman or something? You bored on the road and think you could get your jollies busting into my house?" The man lowered his gun from shoulder to hip level, keeping it aimed the whole time at Andy. "Some kind of crackpot census taker?"

"I sell appliance parts, but not on the road. I have an office in Corpus Christi, a business, actually."

Not knowing what to do with his hands, Andy moved to put them in his pockets. The man with the gun raised the gun to the ready and shook his head no. Andy folded his arms across his chest.

"You don't have no fucking business in Corpus Christi," the man said. He raised his voice, seeming to feel lied to.

"Well, I don't, but my parents do. My dad does," Andy said, trying hard to push the truth past the implausibility of its components. "It'll all be mine someday. Four offices, two warehouses, and a staff of eighteen people who all think I'm an asshole."

The man brought the gun back down to waist level.

"All right. We're getting warmer. Stick with the truth, because being lied to upsets me. No business owner I know wears cheap polyester slacks or paper-thin shirts like that. Is that one of them zip-up ties I've seen at Wal-Mart?"

Andy rubbed his forearms down the middle of the tie on his chest.

"So you're an appliance salesman from Corpus Christi?"

"Parts," Andy said. "I sell appliance parts. Ranges and elements for stoves, motors for washers and driers, coolant frames for ACs. My name is—" Andy started. He raised a hand to offer a handshake with his introduction, but the man raised his gun again.

"I don't want to know your name," he said. "I haven't decided if I'm gonna have to kill you, and I figure it'll be easier to do if I don't know your name."

Andy brought his hand back to the warm fold on his chest but couldn't find the exact spot he'd vacated and so couldn't find the comfort he'd worked it toward.

"So, Mr. Appliance Parts Salesman from Corpus. What the fuck are you doing in my breakfast nook?"

Breakfast nook? Were there breakfast nooks out in the ranchland sticks of south Texas? Part of the appeal of the windows Andy had driven past so many times was the elegant fact of their being hung on a house in a land where, presumably, there was no such thing as even a sunroom. But a breakfast nook?

"I was just looking at the stars," Andy said, his words coming out meekly for how they sounded in his mind.

"Excuse me? Did you say you were looking at the stars?" the man said, incredulous but not disbelieving.

"Yes," Andy said, still ashamed of his response.

"Well, I do suppose that's an appropriate answer," the man said. "But I was wondering more what you're doing here, some one hundred-odd miles away from Corpus Christi, in my home."

"I . . . uh . . . it's a long story," Andy said, confused and daunted by the prospect of tracing what had put him there at the wrong end of a gun in Pawelekville.

"Well, I'll tell you what, Appliance Parts. I've had a long day, a hell of a long day. So I'm gonna sit over here in my living room, where you'll tell me why you're in my home, and I'll decide whether I'll be calling the sheriff to come haul you to jail or a wagon to haul your body to a cabinet in a freezer somewhere."

Andy stood, nervous, about to recite his pathetic truths to a man sitting with a shotgun, butt resting on the seat back next to him, barrels pointed at Andy.

"Do you mind if I sit down? I've had kind of a long drive to get here."

"No," the man said. "You'll stand. See, you broke into my house"—here the man spoke with a singsong, exaggerated twang—"and I'm still a little rubbed raw about that. So you'll stand. And don't worry, I woke up fourteen hours ago to drive a tractor for six hours and then over to San Antonio and back in the truck. I'm still kicking, so I think you'll make it."

"Okay," Andy said. He ran his hands through his sweaty hair. The nerves shaking him were not from the moonlight bouncing off the blue steel that was fixed on him. What was there to say?

"My throat is really dry. Do you think I could get a glass of water?"

"All right, talk." These words were almost shouted. "I'm just about sick of all of this, and you're burning down the bridge of my patient mercy. You can choke to death on your thirst for all the damn I give about your throat. Talk or I end this conversation with a bang. Why the fuck are you in my house?"

"I was just on my way home, and I thought I'd stop."

"Home from the office? That's one hell of a damn commute."

"I live in Austin." Andy's voice trailed here, because he knew he would either have to run down the explanation or sound like a liar.

"Now it's Austin!" The man bolted upright in the seat he'd been slouching in as he shouted this.

"It's always been Austin. I'm from Corpus. I went to school up in Austin. When I finished school, I couldn't find a job, so the parents gave me an assistant manager position at the store."

"So you make this drive every day? Four hours?" The man seemed more confused than anything.

"No. Three and a half. I leave Sunday and stay with my parents till Friday. Then it's back home."

"Why?"

"My wife's in Austin. She has a job there. The Corpus thing was only supposed to be temporary. It's been three years. She won't leave Austin. I haven't found a job there."

The men came to terms with the silence that followed this. The man with the gun sank in his chair a bit and stared off into that space where "huh" resides. Andy shifted on his feet and finally did a sort of squat to get his quads and shins stretched out. He wrapped his arms around his knees and squeezed so hard he made a kind of desperate-sounding groan.

"All right, all right, you fucking weirdo, get up. That doesn't explain why you're in my house. I'm not hearing what I need to hear right now."

"You see, I drive the back roads—181 to 123. And every time I pass by here, I see your house. It's just another house on the side of the road, but your house—"

"The window?" the man said.

"Yes. I've driven by every weekend for the last three years, and every time I do I can't help but be drawn to your window." Here, Andy finally relented to the strain his body was putting on his shaking leg and sank down into an Indian-style seat on the rug in the middle of the hardwood floor. The man, who had no objections to Andy making himself comfortable, sat shaking his head.

"I hate that fucking window," he said.

"Was it there when you bought the house?" Andy asked, making him realize he probably shouldn't have allowed himself comfort in such a situation.

"No, Mr. Appliance Parts/Breaks-into-Houses, it was not there when we *bought* this house. We built the house—designed it, at least. We had a two- and a three-year-old. We wanted them to be able to play outside in the sun, but with the highway so close, we made a sunroom for them to play in. Now they're both older, and we're left with a breakfast nook."

This knowledge restored some of Andy's romance with the place, but they still used that title, breakfast nook, which was as bad as naming a kid Skylarr or Braden or Kucinich.

"How did you know it was the window that got my attention?" Andy asked.

"People in town all do the same thing. I see them passing by, and I feel like a damn fish in an aquarium. Then when I do talk to them at the store, they sound funny. Like they know me. Like they're family or something."

"Oh," Andy said. He had nothing more to say, nothing more to do either, except not be there, which was no longer an easy proposition. He had done this. This was happening.

"But none of them ever broke into my house." The man tilted his head here, and his neck played a drum solo of escaping gases from joints. He took his hand off the trigger of his shotgun, shook tension out of his fingers, and rolled his hand on his wrist. "So either you owe me more explanation or we end it at 'the window made me do it,' and I call the sheriff."

"I wasn't going to break in. The idea was never to break in," Andy started.

"And yet, here we sit," the man said, cutting Andy off.

Andy hung his head here but not from being called out on a logical fallacy. He thought there was no way his words could make sense to the man in front of him. If there were any explanation Andy could even put into words, if he could somehow find the exact elocution to paint a picture of the thoughts and circumstances that brought him to Pawelekville that night, it would make no sense to anyone else. The words would be in a language only Andy understood, and so they would be nonsense.

The man seemed to note his own bullishness. He sat up in his seat, not further readying himself to shoot, but to make of himself a better audience for Andy's explanation.

"Go on," he said.

"You see, I drive by here twice a week, and every time I look at that window. But it's almost like the window's not enough anymore. I drive by and I want to see through the window. I swear," he raised his voice here, desperately, "it's nothing weird. I just drive by and see your house and I expect to see something—like a show. And that's it.

"But today, when I drove by, I had the smallest thought in my head. It was one of those thoughts you get when you've been driving for an hour and a half and you have two more to go. I thought, 'What if I park across the street and wait until I see someone, and then I go introduce myself?' It was a stupid thought, really, but you don't realize how stupid those little thoughts are, because you're not really thinking them. You're really just experiencing what your bored mind is doing to occupy itself."

The man stared silently at Andy. He gave no affirmation of understanding and showed no desire for Andy to go on, but he also did not seem to want Andy to stop talking.

"So that happened. In the thirty seconds it took me to pass your house, I thought that. Then it was gone. That's it. I kept driving for home." This was working. It was making sense, to Andy at least. He could see where his words had brought him in the telling, the realization, of his being there. He was happy to be progressing, but when his mind got to where his words would have to follow him, the truth of the day washed over him. He began to cry. Sitting on the living room floor of the Carpentier house, Andy began to cry. He held his shoulders to try to stop their joining the party of his sobbing over his loss. He raised his index finger to indicate to the man who began stirring uncomfortably in his chair that he just needed a second.

"When I got to Seguin, my phone rang. It was my mom." He cried harder here. After a bit of fighting with himself, Andy continued. "My dad died today."

Andy sat on the floor shaking, crying through eyes shut as tightly as his face would permit. He didn't expect any words of consolation or judgment from the man with the gun, but when he let himself hear the silence they were sitting in, the fact of their sharing the moment without any obligatory back-pats or I'm sorries or phone calls to the authorities bonded the men, it made them more than home owner and intruder, gunman and his righteous kill.

"So I turned around and headed back down to Corpus. I stopped over and got a pork sandwich and a few beers at a place off the highway."

"Red's?" the man asked.

"Yeah."

"That was your second-biggest mistake of the day."

"Tell me about it. The thought came back to me to come and wait for someone to get home and introduce myself when I was there. I was just going to park across the street and wait, but it felt wrong. So I parked a bit up 887 and walked here.

"I wasn't going to break in. No one was here. I found myself on the side of the road standing like a crazy person who was lost in the middle of nowhere. I saw a car coming and I ran. My car was too far. The house was just across the street, so I came."

"Pawelekville," the man said, not giving Andy time to catch his breath. "This is Pawelekville. It's not the middle of nowhere. You're somewhere. You're in Pawelekville."

Andy nodded his assent and stretched his legs out on the rug in front of him. The man with the gun looked away from Andy for the first time. He stared out the window, or maybe he was looking at the window, the cause of so many troubles.

"Where's your wife?" he said. He spoke these words softly, for the first time letting on that Andy's story had affected him, that he cared.

"Austin, I guess. Probably on her way to Corpus. I turned off my phone when my mom called me. I just sat down to a sandwich and beers and any thoughts that were about anything but my dad dying. It's all mine now. The company. The workers. I have to run things now. I don't know if my wife will move to Corpus with me. She hates it." Andy looked at the man for something: an answer, a truth, a way.

"I met my wife in College Station," the man said at the silence between him and the intruder. "I was studying ag business, and she was working on her veterinary degree. When I asked her to marry me, I was afraid she wouldn't take me, my town, my land. But she did. We've been here ever since. I tend the sorghum, she has an office in town. Your wife's not your worry right now." The man looked back at Andy.

"I know. I know. I'm sorry. You do what you have to do right now," Andy said.

"No," the man said. "Your daddy. Your daddy's dead. You need to go take care of your ma and whoever else you got, cause if the castle's yours, I'm assuming you're the oldest."

Andy continued crying.

"So you say your car's up 887?" the man said.

Andy nodded.

"All right," the man said.

He got up from his seat and walked to the entertainment center on which his television sat. He folded down the barrel of his shotgun and pulled out the two shells he had been preparing to explode, sending balls of hot lead shot into and through Andy, his guts and bone fragments going along for the ride and painting the living room horrible shades of traumatic and wrong. He put the shells in his pocket and rested the shotgun atop the entertainment center. He walked across the hall, leaving Andy crying on his living room floor.

When the man came back into the room, Andy again heard the distinct sound of the hammer cocking on a gun. This time, Andy turned right around, not bothering to pause or freeze or grab the sky. There the man stood, a hat on his head, truck keys in his left hand, a shiny nickel-plated handgun in his right.

"Let's get you to your car," the man said.

In the man's truck, Andy buckled his seat belt and rolled down his window. The man put the keys on his lap so that he could shift the gun from his right hand to his left, then he picked up the keys and fired up the engine.

"Your house is really . . ." Andy's voice trailed at not knowing the right word to use. The man cut him off.

"If you say 'quaint,' so help me God I will blow your brains right out my truck window." He sounded tired saying this, like he'd had to say it before—give or take a threat of mortal violence.

"It's nice," Andy said. "Really nice. Fancy even."

The man seemed okay with this appraisal, because he said nothing. He turned onto FM 887.

"You don't ever worry about being out here? So out in the open?" Andy asked. The man said nothing. "You know, like, you don't ever worry about some *In Cold Blood*–type stuff?" Still nothing. "You know, *In Cold Blood*—"

"I know the goddamn book. Hell, it's on my damn bookcase." The man shouted, not angrily, but seeming to want Andy to shut up. "Truman Capote may have been a world-class cocksucker, but he was one hell of a southern writer."

Andy hadn't meant the book. He hadn't even known it was a book. He'd seen the movie on TV late one night. So then he did shut up.

"And who in the hell brings up such a thing when they're sitting with a gun pointed after them, right after they've broken into a house out in the country? That's a dumbshit thing to do, if you ask me. And where the hell is your car?"

They drove on a bit farther. Andy hadn't realized how far off the main highway he'd parked his car. Had he really walked this far? When they got to his car, the man turned his truck around and parked behind it. He turned off the engine.

"Now you listen," he said.

"My name is Andy Johnston," Andy said before the man could continue.

"All right, Andy Johnston, you get in your car and you drive home to your family. Hell, turn on your damn phone and call your poor wife. Do what you have to do. Take care of your stuff, and then have a nice life. But, and I swear it on everything I've got, if you ever come round my house again, I will kill you. The only thing that saved your life tonight is that my family's at the in-laws' and you weren't trying to steal my TV when I walked into that house."

Andy looked out the open window next to him at the different shades of night that made the difference between sky and barren field. He said "okay" over his shoulder and opened the door and stepped to get out of the truck without looking back at the man with the gun. When he got between the front of the truck and the back of his car, he heard the man's door open.

Here, Andy expected, wished for, a bullet to run, hot and spiteful, through the back of his head. He slowed his walk to the point that he was almost not moving and closed his eyes. He felt a great peace within himself at the prospect of it all being about to end, but that peace was interrupted by something heavy and painful. There was too much he would be abandoning. There were too many people waiting for him to show up and make things better, make them right. Peace turned to panic in the course of two or three baby steps in the headlights of the man with the gun.

"Andy," the man called. When Andy turned around, the man said, "My name is Samuel Hernandez." He said his name like someone who couldn't speak Spanish.

"I thought it was—" Andy started, but Samuel spoke up.

"Carpentier." Samuel pronounced it 'car-pen-tear.' Andy had expected it to be the French that rhymed with *papier-mâché*. "It was my mother's name. We got the land from her. She was raised in the shack out behind my house.

"Anyway, I'm sorry for your loss." Before Andy could thank Samuel Hernandez for his condolences, Samuel spoke again. "Now go home and don't come back."

And so, Andy did.

Random Punchlines

At 5:45 a.m., the last of the stragglers had left. Most of the plastic cups that had been strewn about the back and front yards as well as all through the house were in trash bags. All of the vomit had been mopped up from the bathroom floors. It was a pretty successful party. Only one fight had broken out, and it was between two drunken sorority girls, so it was more entertaining than dangerous. Two posters, three CDs, and one keg tap had been stolen. Less than usual. Fourteen kegs of beer had been floated; fifteen gallons of grain alcohol, five fifths of vodka, ten three-liter bottles of Sprite, and fifteen gallons of Hawaiian Punch were distributed evenly among five coolers of punch, of which only half of one cooler remained. All but two members of the fraternity had either taken someone to bed or passed out drunk and alone.

Ryan was the last person awake. He was always the last person awake after parties. He had been working on charming a drugged-out hippie chick into bed with him, but before he could seal the deal she passed out on the couch mid-sentence.

"I must have smoked, like, five bowls before I got to this party, and I don't even know what the fuck those pills I took—" And then she was out.

Ryan laid her down on her stomach and put a half-full wastebasket on the ground next to her head, then went to the backyard to take one last look around. He realized when he fell down the stairs on the back porch that he wasn't in much better condition than the girl he'd left on the couch. He got up, dusted himself off, and leaned onto the backyard bar. He tried to think back on how much he'd had to drink all night and couldn't come up with a number. He needed another one just then. All that was left was punch. He always stayed away from the punch at his fraternity's parties, but the beer was all gone and the night was over, so he poured himself a cup.

It was a rule that all of the members of Ryan's fraternity had to show up at the house at seven o'clock on the night of a party for cleaning and bar set-up. Inside, there was sweeping up the living room, vacuuming the TV room, giving the bathrooms a once-over with a mop, and dealing with the dishes in the kitchen sink and whatever organisms had grown on them; outside, there was wiping down the bar in the backyard, connecting CO_2 tanks in the four-keg kegerator, climbing on a stepladder to clean the leaves and moss that had gathered in the funnels that fed down to the free-standing beer bongs that were never taken down and flushing out any dirt in them with warm, soapy water, and stapling up black tarp onto 4x4 posts planted in the ground around the perimeter of the house's front and back yards. He was tired and had been drinking since set-up was done, around nine o'clock that night.

Before Ryan had his first drink of punch, Tom stumbled out of the house with an unlit cigarette dangling from his lips and a cut over his left eye.

"She fucking hit me." Tom was digging in the pockets of his khaki slacks in search of his lighter. "And with the goddamn ring I bought her. I mean look at me, I'm bleeding. She never drew blood before. All I want is a cigarette, a drink, and for her to not be in that bed when I go back inside."

Tom stood next to Ryan at the bar. Ryan could see the remnants of tears in his friend's eyes and said all that, with his twenty-one years of emotional maturity, he could to help his friend along.

"I don't know who's the bigger bitch, her or you."

Tom rolled his eyes, not even trying to defend himself.

"See, even you know you're a bitch," Ryan continued, reaching into the breast pocket of Tom's black cotton T-shirt, pulling out the Zippo Tom couldn't find. "Shit, man, she's hit you more than once. The bitch is fucking nuts. Why are you even still with her?"

Tom grabbed the lighter from Ryan, offering him a cigarette; he picked up the cup of punch Ryan had poured for himself.

"You have to admit, man." Tom was lighting a cigarette as he spoke. "She's fucking hot. And, I think I love her." He paused for a second, then took a big drink from the plastic cup. "Ugh, why are you drinking this shit? And it's from the bottom of the cooler too. Shit almost made me go blind. Hey, look, you spilled some on your pants."

Ryan looked down at his white slacks, and, not missing a beat, Tom gave him a swift flick to the crotch with the backs of all four of the fingers on his right hand. Ryan bent over and reeled in pain.

"And don't call her a bitch," Tom said.

"Goddamn, man, you got me right on the nut. You drink my punch and then you chotch me in the junk, real classy." Ryan took a few deep breaths before leaning over the bar to draw a new cup of lukewarm punch from the bottom of the dirty ice chest.

Two and a half cups of punch later, the sun was coming up and Tom and Ryan were feeling good.

"I mean, it was in the bag. She was all into me, then she passed out on the couch. One second she was talking, and the next she was out like a light. A really drunk, high light." Ryan rested his head on the bar after saying this.

"Who's a bitch now, you boring asshole?" Tom gave Ryan a punch on his arm. Ryan couldn't tell if Tom was too drunk to realize it, or if he was just mad, but, drunk or not, he didn't take anything off the punch. "You wanna talk about my girlfriend like you're her fucking therapist, and you got girls passing out while you're hitting on them? Faggot-ass hypocrite."

Tom hit Ryan again. This time he hit him so hard that the shorter, smaller Ryan fell to the ground.

It took a moment for Ryan to understand what had happened. Drunk and disoriented, the world spun around him as he tried to pick himself up. Tom grabbed Ryan's hand and pulled him to his feet. All of Ryan's coordination had escaped him, so Tom had to hold him by the arms to steady him. Ryan wasn't any more sober than Tom, so, for a second, it seemed that they were both going to go down. They each grabbed onto a stretch of the bar and stood laughing.

"Thanks, dick." Ryan rubbed his arm in pain, still laughing.

"Damn, your pants are dirty," Tom said, looking down at Ryan's knees. When Ryan looked down to evaluate the damage done to his pants, Tom issued another swift flick to his crotch. Ryan's left hand grabbed for his own crotch. With his right, he punched Tom in the chest, not too hard, but hard enough to knock the drunken man down.

Tom grabbed his chest and gave the ground a pound as he laughed at having gotten Ryan again. He reached a hand up to Ryan, asking for help getting up. Ryan gave him a light kick to the side. "Fuck you. Get yourself up."

With a bit of concentration, Tom was able to stand up. He gave Ryan a slap on the back, and they laughed a bit more before Tom gave Ryan a cigarette and lit one for himself. Ryan took the lighter from Tom, who was swaying standing up. He lit his cigarette and in the silence of the moment that followed took a drink of his punch, looking down at Tom's lighter in his hand. He studied the design of the lighter cover, an orange and green ace of shamrocks card. As he stood swaying back and forth at the bar, the sun now having been up for a while, he concentrated on, regarded, the lighter he held in his hand. After a while, he realized that Tom was talking to him.

"You're the one who's the bitch. So there! How boring do you have to be to put a stoner chick to sleep by talking to her? I mean, you could have fucked her if you, like, showed her something shiny or something." When Ryan looked into Tom's bloodshot, dilated eyes, they both laughed. Tom reiterated, "You're the one who's the bitch."

Tom leaned over the bar and filled up his cup. Ryan watched him, hoping gravity and Tom's drunkenness would provide him with a laugh, but Tom filled his cup without falling over. Ryan looked back down at the lighter in his hand. He thought it was pretty ridiculous. He opened the top and flicked at the flint. He studied the flame the lighter produced, blowing on it and waving the lighter around to watch the flame not die. It was then that Ryan got an idea so perfect as to have been conceivable only in the brilliance that comes after nine straight hours of hard drinking. Lighter still burning in his hand, Ryan looked over at Tom standing—drink in his right hand, cigarette with an inch of ash at its end in his left. He was very near asleep on his feet.

Ryan giggled excitedly at the prospect of his idea coming into chaotic fruition. With one hand, Ryan pulled open Tom's left pant pocket, and with the other he slid in the lit Zippo. Tom didn't notice the fire in his pants right away, as Ryan expected he would. Smoke rose from his pocket before he looked down at his pants. He stared down in hard concentration for a moment, trying to process what he was seeing and feeling. Ryan laughed at the look of fear and panic in Tom's eyes. Tom shook his leg wildly, and Ryan laughed harder.

Caught up in the fun hilarity of Tom freaking out and shaking about like he was having a seizure, Ryan didn't bother to help him out or calm him down. He would intervene when intervention was needed, as went the master plan he'd formulated:

1. Light the Zippo.
2. Slip it in Tom's pocket.
3. Watch him squirm.
4. Help him . . . Pat out the fire . . . Reach into his pocket to take out the lighter . . . Have a drink and a laugh afterward . . . Don't let it get carried away . . .

Step three of Ryan's plan hadn't run its course when step four went out the window. Tom, after his fit of kicking didn't work, did what anyone would do to put out a fire in their pants. He batted both of his hands down at the fire, which still hadn't burnt through the outer layer of his pants. His left hand hit, sending a splash of embers flying from the cigarette he was holding. Then his right hand hit. Ryan heard the sound of the plastic cup cracking as it hit, and saw the bright red contents of the cup spread out onto Tom's pant pocket—some of it traveling up to his shirt and some down to his knee, but most of it landing on his thigh and crotch. Ryan thought, for less than a second, when the cup broke and the punch spread out onto Tom's pants, that the pants were ruined, and momentarily regretted the fact that his joke was going to cost his friend a pair of pants. By the time the last drop of punch landed on Tom's pants, the entirety of what would have been a pinkish-red stain was burning with blue flames that were barely visible in the just-risen Sunday morning sun that was peeking out over the clock tower at the University of Texas just a half mile from where they stood.

Ryan stood in shock as the blue flame of the alcohol burning off turned to a more domestic, less chemistry-class, orange—Tom's cotton pants and shirt were now burning. Tom yelled like he'd been startled by someone hiding around a blind corner. It was a yell that Ryan would remember as being more out of fear and shock than pain. Ryan froze, he couldn't move. He just stood and stared, the sly jackal grin still on his face from his having been laughing at his own joke. Tom looked into Ryan's eyes as he yelled. Ryan's eyes must have registered only blank ineffectiveness in Tom, because he looked only for a second and he ran.

His yells turned to screams as he ran from the bar. It seemed that he was trying to run to the front yard and away from the house, but the tarp that outlined the yard, keeping party crashers out, kept him trapped, running around the backyard rather than in a straight line as people on fire are wont to do.

Ryan snapped out of his hypnosis when Tom passed by the bar on his second lap around the yard. He grabbed Tom from behind, by the shoulder and pulled him to the ground—rolling him over, face-first in the dirt. Tom's screams had woken everyone in the house, except for a couple guys who were heavy sleepers and still drunk from the night before. Several of the fraternity's members stood, crowding the back doorway, watching Ryan tackle their screaming, burning brother.

"Call an ambulance!" Ryan shouted. He lay sprawled out on Tom, trying to cover him like a blanket, but he didn't offer enough surface area to get the job done. Some flames were still coming up from the side of Tom's hip. Ryan patted the fire out and rolled Tom back over. Smoke rose and the smell of burning flesh and the sight of Tom's bloodied, waxlike hip, thigh, crotch, and abdomen made Ryan sick. He took a few steps away, fell to the ground, and vomited out the alcoholic contents of his stomach.

Some of the fraternity members ran out to Tom, thinking they could help but stopping cold when they realized that they probably shouldn't, and couldn't anyway, touch his burnt body. One of them helped Ryan up. Inside, the crowd in the back room had gotten bigger. Ryan heard a female voice from inside offer up to the crowd blocking her view of the backyard, "What happened?"

For the first time, with damning light being cast down on him from the eyes of those uninvolved, Ryan realized that he would have to deal with the consequences of having set a man, his friend and brother, on fire.

Then he heard the panicked voice of one of his fraternity brothers respond. "Tom set himself on fire, Ryan just put him out."

The ambulance got to the house, and the EMTs were told by the members of the fraternity what Ryan had come to accept as the truth of what happened. When his fraternity brothers had asked him what happened he was disoriented, still in shock at having seen, and done, what he did. "The Zippo . . ."

"The Zippo? He lit himself on fire with the Zippo?" One brother had asked him. As crazy as the assumption had been, it was far more logical an assumption to make than the truth. How could one even make the unlikely, accusatory step toward piecing together what had really happened—that Ryan had set Tom on fire?

"Goddamn," the head EMT, a slim, healthy man of about fifty years said to his partner, a scruffy kid no older than Tom or Ryan. "Working in Austin, I've seen drunk college kids stabbed, shot, run over, impaled on gates, drowned in pools, and left bare-assed and passed out in the middle of abandoned farm-to-market roads on the outskirts of town, but this is my first self-immolation."

"These burns are pretty bad." The young EMT pointed out the obvious.

"Call it in, second- and third-degree burns. No field anesthetic, the kid's been drinking," the older man ordered. He began flushing out Tom's burns with saline. Tom was coming into and going out of consciousness at this point with grunts and cries and shouts of pain. There were dirt and grass and baked-on layers of shirt and pants on Tom's wounds. When the cool wash of saline hit his wounds, Tom gave a loud scream and passed out cold from the pain. "He's going to need some major surgery."

After Tom was secured to a gurney and put into the back of the ambulance, the older man asked Ryan, "Do you want to ride with us?" Ryan nodded yes and got in the back. The older man drove and the young EMT rode in back too, tending to Tom.

"So your fraternity brothers said he set himself on fire?" the young EMT asked calmly.

Sitting in the back of the speeding ambulance, rocking side to side, Ryan felt last night all over him. He didn't answer the question.

"And that you put the fire out. So, you're some kind of hero. How'd this all happen?"

Ryan stared out the window of the back door, still not answering.

"Hey." The young EMT raised his voice, forcing Ryan to look up at him. "I asked you what happened."

"We were talking, smoking cigarettes," Ryan started.

"And drinking." The authoritative tone the young EMT used when he interrupted revealed what was going on: Ryan was being interrogated.

"Yeah, we were drinking. I hadn't gone to sleep. He came out after a fight with his girlfriend. We were talking, horsing around, and drinking. I was tired. I spaced out and next thing I know, Tom was kicking around like an idiot."

"And?"

"Smoke came out of his pocket. I didn't understand what was happening at first. Before I knew what to do, he was slapping at his pants. When the punch hit, it went up like gasoline or . . . you know, something flammable." This was the first time Ryan told the lie that was made for him. He looked at the young EMT to see how it was working.

"Like alcohol," the young EMT said with a snort. "Well, he's lucky you were with him. You put him out before too much of him was burned too badly. As it is, the third-degree burns are concentrated in one main area here." He pointed out the rawest, waxiest area of Tom's hip and thigh.

Ryan thought he was going to vomit at the sight, but there was nothing left in him. He saw an evil grin on the young EMT's face. He resented being scared straight by someone his age, but that's not why he felt uneasy. The blackened hole in Tom's clothes, the human grease that had spread out to the parts of the pants that weren't burnt—Tom didn't deserve what he was going through, and he didn't deserve to be blamed for it. Ryan became nauseated and dizzy beyond the initial effects of the rocking ambulance ride on his waning drunkenness and burgeoning hangover. He closed his eyes and tried to calm down. The young EMT kept talking.

"We're almost at the hospital. They'll take him into an emergency room, and they'll take a look at him and see what has to be done. Just stay in the waiting room. A fire marshal will come by later to talk to you. Someone from the department would have come to the scene, but there was a huge apartment fire down on Riverside. They're down there investigating and taking statements. If they don't show up here, they'll contact you at home."

The ambulance stopped and the two EMTs carted Tom into a building and past a door Ryan wasn't allowed behind. Ryan stood, tired and sick, at the back entrance to the emergency room, alone for the first time. He tried to piece together what had happened. He remembered what he'd done, but smaller details, like everything he and Tom had talked about, were already slipping away in the haze of self-induced brain damage and traumatic happenstance. His legs, knees, and back hurt. Not having seen his bed was starting to add to Ryan's general state of feeling shitty. He took a seat in the waiting room and tried unsuccessfully to close his eyes. He leaned his head on the back of the chair and stared up at the ceiling.

Ryan's fraternity brothers and the ER doctor got to the waiting room at the same time. At this point, Ryan was so tired and out of it that he didn't notice either come into the room. The doctor addressed the group of young men that gathered in his waiting room.

"All right, I'm sure you all have a lot of questions. I'll answer all of them shortly, but let me tell you that Mr. King is fine." The doctor said this loudly, to speak over the chatter of Ryan's fraternity brothers, getting Ryan's attention. "We pumped his stomach to get as much of the alcohol as we could out of his system. He's on a mild anesthetic and in stable condition. The concentration of third-degree burns on his side is so great that he will have to have major surgery that we're not equipped to perform here. We're going to fly him over to Galveston."

"Can one of us fly with him?" one of the brothers asked.

"He's going to be flying via helicopter. There is limited room for medical professionals to accompany your friend, and, aside from that, there is a maximum weight capacity. So, no, he'll have to fly alone, but he's anesthetized and won't wake up until after his surgery, so he won't even know you guys weren't with him."

There was a silence. No one had anything else to ask.

"All right, men, I have other patients to see. If you would, contact his family to let them know the situation, or if you'd feel more comfortable, you can leave their contact information with someone at the front desk, and we'll make the call. Don't worry, your friend will be fine." The doctor went back into the emergency room, leaving all of the fraternity brothers overwhelmed.

"Someone needs to call Tom's family, let them know what's happened," one of them said. "And I guess we're going to Galveston. Who's driving?"

Ryan got in a car with some of his fraternity brothers. He sat in the backseat. He still hadn't said anything to anyone since the hospital. From the front seat he heard one of his fraternity brothers on the phone.

"Mr. King? I hope I'm not disturbing you. I'm one of Tom's fraternity brothers. I have some bad news—"

Feeling the car under him making its way east on Highway 290, Ryan felt sleepy. He rested his head on the car window and fell asleep to the sound of his fraternity brother trying to calm a hysterical parent on the other end of the phone. "No, Mr. King. He's fine."

Ryan slept the whole way to Galveston. He was awoken by the fraternity brother who'd called Tom's parents. "We're here."

Ryan no longer felt drunk, and his headache had subsided a bit. He stretched when he got out of the car. "Are we the first to get here?" he asked.

"Yeah. We are," his fraternity brother said, tightening up his face in a cringe. "You smell like someone burned down a bar and pissed on the ashes. There's some mouthwash in the glove box and a T-shirt in the trunk."

Entering the burn unit waiting room, Ryan immediately spotted Tom's parents. Mr. King, tall and slender in cowboy garb from his Stetson down to his ostrich skins, and Mrs. King in a business suit, the work costumes (car dealer and lawyer) neither of them ever took off, but which also paid for the house in Kingwood and the tuition, housing, and allowance for their son.

Ryan had met them at parents' weekends in years past. They recognized him too and Mrs. King rushed over to greet him with a needful hug, seeking solace in the arms of someone else as scared and helpless as she.

"Thank you so much, Ryan. They told us you put out the fire. We owe you so much. We drove right over from church in Houston," Mrs. King said. She pointed at Mr. King. "You remember my husband?"

Ryan nodded and reached forward to shake Mr. King's hand. Ryan's gesture wasn't met and his hand hung for a second waiting, expecting, hoping. Mr. King kept his arms folded and his face straight. He turned away from everyone and said to nobody, everybody: "In my days in the chapter we looked out for each other, made sure nobody got hurt."

"Thomas, not now," Mrs. King said. "Ryan helped when he could. If anyone else could have, they would have."

Mr. King took his seat and said nothing more. None of Ryan's fraternity brothers said anything. Ryan felt criticized, evaluated. And wished he didn't smell of mouthwash and hangover in dirty, grass-stained pants and a T-shirt that was too big on him.

"The doctors finished the first procedure about an hour ago and have started another one. It'll take a while," Mrs. King said, taking her seat next to her husband. "You guys should get some food and try to relax. We appreciate you being here, but there's not much we can do now."

She leaned onto her husband, who put his arm around her. She closed her teary eyes and cried silently. Ryan could see that under the brim of his hat, Mr. King was crying too. He walked toward the cafeteria, toward anywhere away from the waiting room, and his fraternity brothers followed without saying a word.

In the cafeteria, Ryan sat with an untouched cup of coffee in front of him. His fraternity brothers talked to, at, and around him, but Ryan wasn't paying any attention. They tried to take some weight off the situation by joking and acting casually, but no amount of joking could lessen Ryan's burden. Their words melded with the ringing of registers, the shuffling of chairs, the scrape of fork on plate, CNN on the TV in the corner, and the other insignificant chatter in the cafeteria.

"He lit himself on fire. I put him out," Ryan thought. Selling himself the lie so that he could tell it believably. "He lit himself on fire. I put him out. I didn't mean to hurt him. He lit himself on fire. I put him out. It was an accident. I couldn't have known. He lit himself on fire. I—"

"Ryan." The fraternity brother sitting across from him slapped the table. "Are you going to come with us?"

"What? Where?" Ryan said.

"To my parents' house. It's not far, just over in Humble. We can meet the other guys there and wait for news. What are we going to do here?" He looked exhausted. Ryan realized he wasn't the only one who'd had a long night.

"No, I'll stay here. I'll call if anything happens."

No one asked Ryan twice. They gave him pats on the back and knuckle bumps and handshakes, and they were off.

After some time alone, Ryan finished his now-cold coffee. Went to the restroom to wash his face and kill some more time before joining Mr. and Mrs. King in the waiting room. He walked to the waiting room and decided he wasn't ready to face them, so he stepped outside for some fresh air.

There was a bench outside the hospital entrance, but someone was sitting there, talking into a Bluetooth headset. Not seeing anywhere to sit, Ryan thought to go back inside but stopped when he heard something that made him linger.

"So I'm at the hospital in Galveston because my cousin set himself on fire." The man sitting on the bench was wearing a black fitted polo shirt, grey wool slacks, and polished black loafers. He was dressed for work on

Sunday. "Yeah, he set himself on fire. I don't know. My aunt said it was after a fraternity party, so I figure he was shit-faced drunk and did it on a dare. I know. I mean, he's spoiled, but he's never been this much of a fuckup. Yeah. My mom's out of town, so she asked me to come check up on my aunt and uncle. Yeah. Just let Ken know. I'll have my part of the report done and sent to you by tonight. Fucking family, right? All right, thanks. Bye."

Ryan walked inside before Tom's cousin saw him.

". . . I didn't mean to hurt him. It was an accident. I didn't mean for any of this to happen . . ."

Ryan entered the waiting room and sat across from Mr. and Mrs. King. Shortly thereafter, Tom's cousin walked in. Once again, Mr. and Mrs. King stood to welcome their guest. This time Mr. King administered his own hug.

"Scott, you shouldn't have come down here. We're just waiting. You could have come later." Mr. King's tone was different. Ryan was now all alone.

"Uncle Thomas, Mom called and wanted me to make sure her little brother was okay. Besides, they called me down to the office to finish up a file. So I'm not really missing out on anything." He smiled. His joke broke the tension in the room. Everyone sat.

"This is Ryan. He put your cousin out. If he hadn't reacted like he did, this would all be so much worse." Mrs. King looked up at Ryan.

"Thank you for your help, Ryan. I'm Scott." They nodded at each other. Mr. King looked up at Ryan and nodded too.

Scott looked at Ryan. "So what exactly—"

Hearing these words, Ryan shuddered, knowing what he would have to do. Saying it to the young EMT was one thing, but lying to these people—Ryan wished he had left with his fraternity brothers. Scott didn't even finish his sentence when the doors to the operating room opened. The doctor who walked out looked drained. Her shoulders hunched over and her face flush, it was obvious she'd earned her money for the day. She walked over to the King family and Ryan. Everyone stood to hear what she would say.

"All right, we've finished the second of his major surgeries. We only have one more procedure, a minor one, to do today." Sighs of relief were let out, and Mr. and Mrs. King grabbed each other's hands, but the tired doctor wasn't done talking. "This is definitely all good news, and your son is doing quite well, under the circumstances. But you need to be prepared for a long rehabilitation period. While the burns to his groin aren't so bad as to require graft surgery, he will have very limited mobility and require long-term medical care. Nothing looks life-altering, long-term. He'll lead a normal life, you'll get grandchildren, or at least have the chance. But these next fifteen to eighteen months are going to be painful and taxing for everyone involved."

"What's the treatment going to entail? What can we expect to happen to our son?" Mr. King asked, sounding defeated and hurt.

"I can't answer these questions specifically about your son's case. When he has time, I'll have Dr. Donovan, our rehab specialist, come talk to you all. Until then, a hospital counselor will come by to talk to you. Now, the main reason I've come out here is because with the time the extra tests and consultation have taken, Tom has come to. He's asking to see his parents, and, in light of what's happened, I think it'd be fine if you guys went in to talk to him for a bit." The doctor was smiling now, trying to infuse the proceedings with some positivity.

"Of course." Mrs. King looked like she was forcing her shock to wear a happy grin at the chance to see her son. Ryan hoped he'd be able to go too, but wasn't going to ask. He was about to sit back down when Mrs. King said, "C'mon, boys, let's go see him."

The doctor explained that he wasn't going to be a pretty sight and that he would be loopy from the drugs. Only two people would be allowed into the room at a time. Mr. and Mrs. King and Ryan were taken to sinks and told to scrub their arms and hands. Scott didn't want to see his cousin in such a state, so he waited. Before Mr. and Mrs. King went in to see their son, they were instructed by the doctor not to touch him or anything else in the room. Simple instructions that the doctor said would be hard to follow.

Ryan waited in the hallway, feeling itchy in his sterilized smock and hat and rubber gloves, with Scott. After a bit of silence, Scott spoke to Ryan.

"You know, we're all very grateful to you for helping my cousin. I need to tell you that, because I don't know what my aunt and uncle are going to do or say after hearing that doctor or seeing Tom on that bed in there." He seemed to expect Ryan to say something in response. When Ryan remained silent, he kept talking. "You know, when I heard about this I laughed. I joked and I laughed. If it all hadn't happened this way, I'd probably still be laughing to myself. I just feel bad."

Ryan looked at Scott in his business clothes and remembered what he'd overheard outside. Scott probably did feel bad, but his little awkward silence-filling confession angered Ryan. Whether it was politicking or even in hope of absolution, it was selfish.

"Yeah," Ryan said. "I'd feel bad too."

Scott stopped talking. They waited.

After a while, Mr. and Mrs. King came out of the room tear-soaked and shaking.

"He looks really bad, son," Mr. King said to Ryan, who was going in alone.

Ryan nodded. He didn't say that Tom couldn't possibly look as bad as he did in the backyard, smoke coming off of him, skin bubbling, flame-broiled.

He walked into the room that was smaller than he expected. Tom was wrapped up in white bandages turned bled-through pink. He was connected to machines and monitors. His head was resting on the pillow behind him. Ryan came to the side of the bed and looked down on Tom, whose eyes were closed.

"Hey, bro, it's me," Ryan said.

Tom opened his eyes and looked at Ryan. He didn't say anything.

"How are you, man? How are you feeling?"

Tom closed his eyes and opened them slowly. "I don't feel anything, man."

"Do you know where you are?" Ryan asked.

"My parents say I'm in Galveston, but that doesn't make any sense. I think they're lying." Tom looked like he was going to keep talking, so Ryan waited. "What're you doing here in Galveston?"

"Tom, do you remember what happened last night?" Ryan asked, scared of what Tom's answer was going to be, but, here in the disinfected stink of the hospital room, in the ugly glow of its fluorescent lights bouncing off of its taupe walls, he was fully prepared to face whatever trouble would come from it.

"Yeah, man, I do. Fuck you." Tom turned his head to look right at Ryan, who was cut deep by the response.

"Listen, man, I'm so sorry for what happened. I'm so sorry. Listen—"

Tom cut him off. "Fuck you, Ryan. You're the bitch. Talking shit to me."

Ryan didn't quite understand what was happening, "What are you talking about, Tom?"

"Where's Beth? I want to see Beth."

Ryan realized they weren't having the same conversation. "She's on her way here with the other guys. She'll be here soon."

"Good. I love her, Ryan. I fucking love her, man."

"I know you do. I'm sorry about last night. I didn't mean to . . . I didn't mean to hurt you."

"I know you didn't, bro," Tom said. He rested his head again and closed his eyes. "I'm so tired. I think I'm going to sleep. Thanks for coming. Tell my parents I'm okay. And tell them we're not in Galveston."

"All right, take care." Ryan looked at Tom in the bed, knocked out. Tom probably didn't even hear him say goodbye.

Ryan stood there in the hospital room before joining the King family in the hallway and walking with them out to the waiting room, where he would call his fraternity brothers and let them know what was happening, and where he would have to answer everyone's questions about what had happened. He was readying to do that. He closed his eyes and stood letting the sound of the beeps that marked his friend's heartbeats tell him how bad the joke could have gone. The beeps were steady, and Ryan wondered how many beeps he would hear if he were connected to one of these machines all day every day. Just out in the real world, living and doing regular things. Beep . . . Beep . . . Beep . . . Beep . . . The sound of the machine put a half minute's drunken planning of a bad joke into perspective. Tom would keep going. The machine would keep beeping. His heart would keep beating.

Ryan left the room ready to face the Kings and his fraternity brothers and Austin's fire marshal when he got back home. He just needed to remember, "He lit himself on fire. I put him out."

Closeness to Taste

William started giving pieces of himself to the hungry citizens of Austin, Texas, the first time he prepped dough at PizzaTex, which, incidentally, was the first time he had handled any food at the shop, aside from pulling pies off the conveyor belt on the shop's only oven with the shop's only peel, an ancient, long-handled punisher that would inject slivers of splintering wood into the hands of any unfortunate cook or, as in William's case, delivery driver who used it. But when William pulled pies off the belt, the deal was quick. He didn't even have to wash his hands, as Robert, his short, fat, crew-cut Armenian boss pointed out on William's second day.

"What the fuck are you doing?" When Robert yelled this, William could smell the whiskey on his breath over the extra-large veggie supreme with extra jalapeños and bell peppers that was about to fall off the belt. "You don't need to wash your hands when you're using the peel. Do you touch the pizza? I don't think so. Just take it out, slide it on the box, and get the fuck out of here."

The day before, William had walked in to inquire about the open delivery driver position he had seen advertised on the shop's window. Robert asked his name, age, and whether he was licensed to drive. When William said yes, Robert grabbed a hot bag that was sitting atop the oven, which was right behind the counter, and handed it to him.

"This is going to Medical Arts. You know where that street is?" Robert didn't give William a chance to answer. "The price and address are on the slip on the pizza box. You got cash?" William, still confused by the red-hot bag that lay on the counter in front of him, shook his head no. "Here's ten dollars." Robert pulled ones out of the register. "Pay it out of your tips at the end of the night. We're open till two tonight; you'll have to stick around to clean up after. Call if you have any questions."

William grabbed the bag and took off for the apartment specified on the receipt in the hot bag. He drove carefully, as if he were transporting hazardous waste or a newborn home from the hospital. He'd walked into the shop on a whim. He'd had nothing to do and remembered the sign in the window of the shop he drove by nearly every day. Driving up Lamar in rush-hour traffic, William was excited by the job's potential for spontaneous interactions with people. It was those fantasies, part porno and part sitcom, that had interested him in the delivery job to begin with. He knocks. They open. Talking. Joking. Money exchanging hands. Who doesn't like answering the door for the pizza guy? He found the apartment and didn't feel uneasy until he knocked on the door. He didn't have a uniform, he couldn't answer any questions the customer might have, and he didn't know the number to PizzaTex.

A woman opened the door, young. She wore sweats and a T-shirt, but her hair and makeup were still done up from her day at the office. She grabbed the pizzas, handed William a twenty and two ones, and closed the door before he could say thanks. Not exactly what he'd expected, but William didn't blame the lady. She looked tired. He wanted to massage her tired feet and listen to her latest anecdotal evidence that her boss is a clueless ass. He settled for the half smile she forced before closing the door. William had delivered his first pizza.

Driving back, William was happy with himself for having gotten the job. He hadn't worked since he lost his job answering phones at Dell, and that was three months ago. His call times ran over too often, and he was handed his walking papers. He hadn't minded too much. The job was too impersonal. He had scripts to follow for the customers, and cubicle walls cutting him off from his coworkers. It was almost as lonely as home. In his new job, he felt he might have found something that suited him. All he needed to do was ask Robert for specifics about his pay.

On his first day, William delivered twelve pizzas, cleared $35 in tips, after paying Robert back, and learned that his pay was $5/hr plus tips and that PizzaTex opened at three thirty in the afternoon. On his second day, he pulled his first pizza off the oven belt, shed the first drops of blood he would at PizzaTex when the peel introduced itself to him, and was yelled at for washing his hands. It wasn't until his third week at PizzaTex that William prepped dough and started the cycle of giving that would spread him, his essence, all over Austin and all over the world.

It was a Wednesday. Wednesdays were slow at PizzaTex. There were two things keeping the business afloat: the shop's hours, open until two in the morning on weekdays and four on weekends, and the fact that the store's delivery area covered all of Austin. William had been sent on a run to an older couple at an apartment complex on Grand Avenue Parkway at four thirty in the afternoon, right after he'd come in to work. It took him an hour to get there, and the old man who opened the door William knocked on initially refused to take the pizza but had a change of heart when he looked at the sweaty, nervous state William was in. He even made a show of putting a shiny quarter—without an ounce of irony in his porous bones, shrunken by time, by having lived in another time, a simpler one when a dollar meant something, and a quarter so much more than one-quarter of that mean- ing—in the breast pocket of William's shirt. He gave William a nod that, coupled with the quarter, was meant to calm William down and show ap- preciation for the stock the young man obviously placed in a job well done.

William placed his palm on his pocket, above his heart, and gave a closed-eyed smile, not speaking for fear of the emotions his voice would have betrayed if he had. The old man smoked sweet pine tobacco from a jade pipe and had the words Semper Fi tattooed on his forearm. Driving back, William tried to calculate whether the man was young enough to have fought in Vietnam, as he was certainly old enough to have fought in Korea. He would have led men into the jungle; William would have followed.

William returned to the shop at six o'clock frustrated from having crawled to and from his destination on a packed I-35, and sweaty because it was the middle of summer in the middle of Texas and his truck didn't have AC.

He walked into the shop as Robert wrapped up a call with the only person who had ordered since the marine and his wife on Grand Avenue called in, two hours prior. "Go to the kitchen. You're doing dough; Justin'll show you how."

William went into the kitchen, which housed all of the raw materi- als that went into making pizza. All of the toppings were sliced, and all of the dough and sauce were mixed, in the kitchen. Justin was standing over the dough kettle. William had never worked with Justin, just passed by him coming in from and going out on runs. He looked equal parts menacing and ridiculous, with his ball-ended horseshoe septum ring and his hair: high-wedge-shaved on the sides and long on top, with a bleached-blond streak running up the middle of his hair, where a Mohawk would be, sur- rounded by greasy black hair. He wore long black denim shorts and a cutoff Slayer T-shirt with cartoonish satanic imagery on it. He was tall and slightly muscular, but more lanky than anything else. "You wanna help me with this shit?" he asked sleepily.

The kitchen wasn't air-conditioned, and while the oven was in the front room of the shop, the heat in the kitchen was stifling enough that when working in the back, William and Justin would make unnecessary trips into the walk-in freezer to cool off. The dough was mixed in a fifty-gallon steel kettle by a huge mechanical corkscrew. Transferring the dough made by fifteen gallons of raw materials from the kettle to the prepping table should probably have been a four-person job, but there were only ever two people in the shop (a driver and a cook) during afternoons and evenings, and due to the fact that most orders came at night, particularly when the bars let out, ingredient prepping was done then. Once the dough was moved, it had to be cut, weighed, and put on a tray to be placed in the walk-in for later use.

Justin raised the corkscrew mixer out of the kettle and reached in, grabbing half of its contents. William followed his lead and grabbed at the other half of the flour-powdered, sticky blob. Justin gave a three-count and they lifted the dough out of the kettle and carried it to the prepping table. Winded from the exertion, and still wet with sweat from his drive up 35, William wiped his brow before grabbing a cutter and hacking at the dough.

"You were gone a really long time," Justin said. He didn't have to look down at the dough he was cutting and could probably have gotten by without the scale to weigh the chunks he cut out. He seemed to work by feel, streamlined and machinelike. His hands and fingers knew the feel of 16 oz. medium, 22 oz. large, and 26 oz. extra-large pizzas in their embryonic states. "Where'd you go on that last run?"

"Grand Avenue Parkway," William said. He had to concentrate on what he was doing. Cut, wipe sweat from his brow, weigh, wipe sweat from his brow, cut off more to add to the dough on the scale, wipe sweat from his brow.

"That's technically in Pflugerville, man. You gotta say something next time. If we get a call from Oklahoma, Robert'll send us on the run. We only cover Austin. You gotta say something." Justin shook his head as he slapped the weighed globs of dough into domes and placed them on trays. He had filled three trays already; William was just finishing his first. "Welcome to the seedy underground of the pizza industry."

Justin put his finished trays of dough mounds into the freezer and was sent out on a run, leaving William to finish prepping the remaining dough. He was getting better at it, but still working slowly. Standing at the prepping table, having finished the dough, William put down the cutter and rested for a minute. He ran his hands through his wet hair, wiped them on his pants, and picked up his trays to take into the freezer. Hands full, he had to kick the door open. After his struggle with the door, William dropped the trays down on a shelf in the freezer. When he did this, beads of sweat dripped from his face onto a few mounds of dough that were on the top tray.

He looked down at the tray. Even though they had washed their hands, both William and Justin had been sweating, and some of that sweat had to have run down their arms to their hands and onto, into, the dough, William reasoned. Nothing was different now, except that he saw the sweat fall on it, rather than it having crept in. He stared at the mounds of dough on which his sweat had fallen, feeling the cold air on the wet cotton of his shirt and soaked-through jeans, thinking. He couldn't think for too long; Robert shouted for him from the front room. There was food to be delivered.

That night, William opened the door to his efficiency apartment and was met by the nagging whine of his cat, Cat. Cat had tipped over his water, and his food bowl was empty. William cleaned up the water and refilled Cat's bowls. He sat on his bed, a futon that he no longer bothered to prop up as a sofa—what for? He warmed some garlic bread and his half of a medium meatlover's in the microwave he could reach from the end of his bed. He and Justin had split the food after a drunken customer had refused to take it. The customer had refused to pay William the $26 Robert charged for it.

After hours, when people were getting home from clubs and parties, Robert would adjust the price of an order according to how drunk a caller sounded. He would quote them one price over the phone and write down another on the receipt, sending his drivers out to find out whether or not the customers would notice. The drunks usually paid, but sometimes they rebelled against his monopoly. William didn't blame them and even liked the ones who, like the one that night, still gave him a tip for his time.

William's apartment was a mess of pizza boxes. That was all the food he was eating, two meals a day. When there were no takeback pizzas at the end of the night, after Robert had left for home, William and Justin would cook a pie to split—Justin was on the PizzaTex diet too. They wouldn't make anything too extravagant, just maybe an extra-pepperoni. William's work hours kept him asleep until well after noon. He would wake up, heat some pizza, and try to find something on TV to pass the time until he had to go in to work.

William wasn't too tired after work, but still he went to sleep after a slice of the meatlover's. He lay in bed, Cat nuzzling his ribs, thinking. He had work tomorrow, work the next day, the day after that off—he'd call his brother then. It was times like these when it all caught up to him, all of the nothing of his life. In his loneliness, he always thought of Jesus. When his parents sent him to "counseling," back in school, Father James always ended their sessions by telling William that whatever was ailing him was nothing compared to Jesus's suffering.

No friends? *Jesus's best friends betrayed him and denied him and then built a church in his name. God bless the few who did the latter.*

Depressed? *Jesus bore the pain of the world on his shoulders.*

Lonely? *Imagine how Jesus felt—beaten, bleeding, and betrayed on the floor of a Roman outpost holding cell.*

And it was this shame-by-comparison brought on by self-pity that William had been taught at Sts. Cyril and Methodious School, the best coping mechanism their best "counselor" had to offer a depressed student, which brought William's thoughts to Christ, then to pizza, and then to the world. The idea was huge and exciting, but William knew excitement was hard to come by, so he slept on it. He took a deep breath of Christ, smiled, and fell asleep as close to happy as he'd been in as far back as he could remember.

When he got to work the next day, William went to the freezer and saw that the dough he and Justin had prepped the day before was gone. He smiled, already feeling connected to dozens of people.

"You believe that?" Justin said, walking into the freezer. "We had such a crazy stretch of orders last night, and of course my last run was ten pies down to Onion Creek. Fucking typical. And now we have to prep more dough and cut toppings."

When Justin added the ingredients to the kettle, William paid close attention.

"You like metal?" Justin asked, working slowly.

"Yeah, sure. As much as any other kind of music."

"That's badass, man. I love metal. I'm all about it. And all kinds too. I'll listen to thrash, black, death, doom, grindcore, stoner—I dig it all. I'm starting a band. We're called Angelfuck. Badass, right? Angelfuck." Justin said the name in his Cookie Monster metal voice.

"Well, yeah. I mean, it kind of doesn't make sense," William said.

"What doesn't make sense about Angelfuck? Angel. Fuck. Fuck angels. Angelfuck."

"It has a ring to it, but you can't fuck an angel. They're not humans."

"What, so it's like a cross-species thing? Because you can fuck across species, you just can't procreate." Justin stopped what he was doing and looked at William.

"Angels aren't a species. They're celestial bodies—intangible, beyond our perception. They only take human form if they need to speak to someone, and they usually only do that in dreams." William's voice trailed and he felt stupid for having sparked a conversation about angel fucking.

"I guess that makes sense," Justin said, nodding his head in agreement. "It still sounds badass. It's the title of an old Misfits song."

Justin went back to adding the last of the dough ingredients. He set the corkscrew and cranked on the machine. William debated bringing up the epiphany he'd had the night before.

"Did you take chemistry back in high school?" he asked Justin over the noise of the machine's motor.

"Yeah, doesn't everyone?"

"Well, there was this thing my chemistry teacher said in high school. He said that there are so many molecules in one breath that the last breath that Jesus Christ breathed on the cross expanded, and the molecules it contained are still in the air."

"You have that wrong," Justin said, turning off the machine when the ingredients were mixed to dough.

"What, the chemistry? I don't have a formula or anything, but if you think about it—"

"No, it's Julius Caesar. The lesson is about Julius Caesar's last breath. My father teaches chemistry in Houston," Justin said. He started pulling the dough off the sides of the kettle, and William joined him.

"All right . . . 1 . . . 2 . . . 3 . . . ," William counted and they lifted. "But that doesn't matter. If it's true for one, it's true for the other. And if it's true, we're breathing in Jesus right now."

"But we're also breathing in Julius Caesar . . . and Hitler too." Justin hacked at a piece of dough. "And how can you be sure that we're getting any of the molecules from that last breath, anyway? The point of the lesson is that there are tons of molecules in the atmosphere."

William started in on the dough, quiet, thinking. "But Jesus was the human embodiment of God. So his breath was divine. And it wouldn't be just his last breath. It'd be every breath he ever breathed that we're breathing."

"Well, it'd be every one of Hitler's breaths too, and every ungodly monster you can think of. But I guess you have me on the divinity thing. So, yeah, along with all of the breath of everyone who's come before us, we breathe in some God air," Justin said, carrying a tray to the freezer. "But doesn't that mean that we breathe in everyone who's alive and breathing?"

"Yes!" William put down his dough cutter. "That's what I realized. We're all connected—you, me, and everyone alive and dead."

"That's pretty deep, man."

"And all that we ever really try to do is make those connections closer. To touch up against and become part of as many people as possible."

"Like sex? To advance humanity, all that jazz?"

"It's that." William took a tray to the freezer. Coming out, he said, "And it's so much more than that. Just to give pieces of ourselves to the world and know that by giving pieces of ourselves, we're being spread by everyone who takes us. It's a cycle, a beautiful cycle."

Justin nodded his head and continued hacking at the dough. The two of them worked quietly, until Robert screamed for Justin to start cooking three pies for an order he'd just gotten. William continued working. Scooping sweat off his brow and kneading it into the dough. He scooped and scooped, but the sweat didn't seem enough. He dragged his hands through his hair for the sweat and grease that had accumulated and saw white flakes of dandruff fall onto the counter before him. He leaned over the counter so that his head hovered over the mound of dough and began shaking the dandruff out of his hair onto the dough. It snowed down onto the blob, which would be cut into at least fifteen mounds of dough to be rolled, topped, baked, and then served to people at the farthest corners of Austin, Texas, who would share it with everyone they know, meet, cross, and never think to imagine.

In the weeks that followed, William had been taught every aspect of cooking pizzas at the shop. From making the dough from scratch; to prepping the toppings, cutting the vegetables big enough to cover a pizza, but still small enough to look like a lot; to rolling, beating, and topping pizzas to place in the oven, William could do it all. Business had gotten so bad at the shop—mainly because of Robert pushing his overcharges too far and having a short temper with the callers at all times, no longer only after the bars let out, cursing them out and banning them from the shop—that Robert had fired all of his workers but William and Justin. They were running the shop every day, open to close.

One day, William was chopping onions in the back. He had devised a method of chopping onions wherein he placed the cutting board on a stack of seven dough trays so that it would be at his eye level. He found that this was optimal in drawing the most tears. Halfway through an onion, William had tears streaming down his face, onto the onions and whatever vegetables needed cutting that day. William heard Justin come into the store from a run. He took the cutting board off the trays and wiped his eyes.

"I've been thinking about that conversation we had about Jesus and being connected and all that," Justin said, popping a piece of chopped onion in his mouth. The two had been spending a lot of time together, particularly during closing time, when they would talk, mainly about heavy metal and anything else Justin had in mind, while mopping up the shop. "The members of Kiss each put drops of their blood in the ink that was used to print their comic books in the '70s. They said it was to give part of themselves to their fans. It's like you were saying about the cycle."

William was pleasantly surprised to hear that Justin had been thinking of their conversation; he hadn't brought it back up since they first talked. "Yes, that's exactly what I'm talking about."

"And the cover of one of Metallica's albums is cow blood mixed with a dude's jizz. So that's kind of the same thing."

"Was it one of the band members' semen?" William asked, excited.

"No, but they said that's why they chose it. Because it was art. Like, I guess they knew the guy was trying to give himself to the masses. I mean, I guess it's not the same thing. But, whatever, it's from an album after they cut off their hair and their balls," Justin said, and then popped another piece of onion in his mouth. "But there's this band from Norway. They're called Mayhem. What happened was that their singer decided to kill himself. I mean, he was all in. He slit both his wrists and then blew his head off. Fucking gruesome. The guitarist of the band found his body and took a picture of the scene. He made it the cover of their next album—blood, brain matter, and all."

William put down the knife, shaking his head. "That's hardly what the cycle is about."

"Yeah, I know. But what he also did was pick up pieces of the singer's skull. He made necklaces out of the pieces to give to the other guys in the band and to fans and friends. You know, so they could all have pieces of their old friend."

"That's a totally unimaginative, graphic example, but exactly what I'm getting at." William scooped the chopped onions into a small tray, took them to the refrigerator on the topping line. Justin followed him to the front of the shop.

"And to top it all, he had scooped up some of the brain matter and put it in the freezer. After some time had passed, he put it in a pot and made some soup that he and his band members ate. That kind of sharing will get you closer to someone than fucking. You're eating part of someone, taking them into your system for nutrients. That's connection. Right?"

William was quiet. He closed the topping line cooler, then wiped the top of it off with a rag. A half thought of sharing his sharing with Justin entered his mind. Just a half thought, because before his mind could think it, he shot it down, knowing it would only mean trouble and embarrassment, despite the fact that Justin had become a real friend. Above jeopardizing that friendship, William feared losing his ability to share himself with Austin—with mankind. He felt interrogated, found out. He looked at the clock on the wall. Four thirty.

"No, Justin, that's disgusting. It's wrong and disgusting. There are no calls on the board. I need to run to the store to get some flour. If we get any orders, cook them, and if I'm not back when they're ready to go, drive them out. Just lock the door when you go." William threw his apron under the counter, grabbed a twenty from the register, and left Justin standing silent in the kitchen.

A month later, William gave Justin a pat on the back and locked the door after Justin left the shop. "All right, man, I'll see you tomorrow. Don't forget about my show this Friday. Angelfuck, live at Redrum!" Justin used his Cookie Monster voice for the announcement.

It was 1:45 on a Wednesday night. The calls had come in slow that night, so William had told Justin to head home. He took the phone off the hook and mopped the shop as quickly as he could. He had taken to coming into work early so he could spend quality time with the ingredients, but, since it was a slow night, William figured he could stay behind after closing up. He took trays of dough out of the freezer and laid them out next to one another. Taking his time with each, he shook dandruff onto each tray. When he had finished that, he stacked them back up in the freezer.

Then he chopped an onion, not bothering to stack up trays to bring it to eye level, opting instead to lay his head on the counter, inches from the chopping. When the tears were good and falling, he let a few drops fall onto all of the toppings—the onions, tomatoes, peppers, and olives.

When he was done with the vegetables, he went to the refrigerator and took out the next day's bag of pepperoni, wiped the remaining tears and sweat from his face and head, and carefully, as if laving water onto a baby in a sink, rubbed them onto the meat—taking care to rub every Eucharist-sized piece. This was the topping that would give William to the second-most people. To ensure that he would be spread as far as possible, William took a paring knife and ladle into the freezer.

He took the tops off of the three huge pots of pizza sauce he and Justin had made from bulk cans of tomato sauce and spices earlier that day. He took the paring knife and stabbed a small hole into his forearm (he had already mangled up all of his fingertips and was seeking out new, inconspicuous places on his arms to puncture). He milked the small wound until the blood flowed freely, wiped it off, and let one big, fresh drop fall into each pot. He could see the drops, big as dimes, standing out deep and dark on the bright red sauce. He wiped his forearm, then used the ladle to stir each pot thoroughly enough to where he felt like his blood had touched every particle of sauce in each pot. When he was done, he looked at the sauce in each pot and could swear they were at least half a shade darker than they were before he became a part of them. He topped the pots, closed the freezer, then checked the rat traps before putting the phone back on the hook and shutting down PizzaTex for the day.

When he drove up to work the next day, William saw Justin smoking a cigarette on the hood of his car in front of the shop.

"Did you forget your keys again, angelfucker?" William asked.

"Nope. The key don't work." Justin shook his head, dropping ash on his chest.

"What do you mean?" William tried his key and saw that the lock had been changed. He looked in the shop and saw that the cash register was gone. "What happened?"

"We've been shut down." All of the blood left William's head when Justin said this. He leaned on the hood of his truck, feeling like he was going to throw up. "Robert hasn't gotten any of the store's profits to the owner in three weeks, and apparently he's gone to Armenia. Asshole."

Dizzy from fighting hyperventilation, William looked as confused as he felt. "Wait, I thought he owned the place."

"Yeah, so did I. The fucker acted like he did. But he didn't and we've been shut down. The owner lady called me and I said I'd let you know. We're getting a month's severance. One hundred sixty hours at $5/hour. So we're getting shit." Justin looked at William. "You all right, man? You look sick."

William, having just gotten over the shock of thinking he'd been found out, now had to deal with the fact that he was without his connection to the world. A hole opened up in him and began its unending expansion. He felt it growing and pushing beyond the bounds of his ribs and outside of him.

"It's gonna be all right, William, you'll get a job." Justin got off of his hood and stood next to him. "And tomorrow you'll come out to my show, and we'll get trashed and rock out to some metal." He gave William a playful punch on the arm. William felt Justin's heat, the pressure of the blow, and wanted the whole of his own body to wrap itself into a ball of that sensation.

"Yeah, I guess you're right," William said, still shaken.

"So relax. Go home and go to bed, or do whatever you do at home, and you'll feel better. I've gotta go now, but I'll see you tomorrow." Justin reached out his hand, and William could have cried; it felt so wonderful to merge his mass with his friend's if even only for a quick shake up and down.

William got home and sat on his bed. Cat greeted him with a meow and crawled into the cool darkness under the bed. William looked around the room—the entirety of his home. The pizza boxes and dirty clothes that were strewn about the place served to oppress William, to remind him that the mess was all he had. It was five o'clock in the afternoon, and the sun was still high in the summer-turned-autumn sky. The room was hot, but William didn't get up to turn on the AC. He just sprawled out on his bed, kicked off his shoes, and lay there for the hours it took him to fall into a sweaty, fully clothed sleep. He woke up after sunset, then a few hours later, and twice in the middle of the night, but he resisted that in him which told him he was done with sleep, and he lay there until the next morning, when he got out of bed with a sore back and a headache.

That day, he looked for a job online. There was nearly nothing he wanted and even less that he was qualified for. He heated the last three slices of the last pizza he'd eat for free and ate them in silence in front of the computer, imagining that he could taste his special contributions to the pie.

It wasn't until he was about to give up on searching that William found a job that he thought would suit him. He didn't have any experience in the particular field he was applying for, but he figured his time at PizzaTex couldn't hurt. He called and was given an interview time for the Monday coming up. He was almost happy, but he knew better. He wondered if Jesus had ever been laid off, but aren't carpenters usually self-employed?

That night, William drove downtown and walked around for almost half an hour before he found the bar Angelfuck was playing. He walked into the bar and was impressed by the room. It had a high, arched ceiling, like it had been converted from an old church, probably Baptist or Evangelical. He sat at the bar with a beer and looked up at the ceiling, feeling simultaneously close to and far away from God in an old church that housed the music of the devil.

William saw Justin at a table and walked over to greet him.

"William! I was just talking about you," Justin said. "I was telling everyone about work." He sat at a table with four men and a woman. All of the men were in their thirties, dressed like Justin with hairstyles of varied ridiculousness.

"Yeah, I know. It was pretty—" William began but was interrupted when the MC called on the mic—"Angelfuck to the stage, you've got five for soundcheck."

"We'll all talk later when we get trashed," Justin said. "Right now we must crush some skulls." He and the other men at the table got up and walked onstage, leaving William standing at the table with the woman, who motioned for him to join her.

"I'm Mary. My brother's Isaac, the drummer. Nice to meet you." She held out her hand and shook William's. He was warmed by the firm grip of her soft hand.

"Nice to meet you too, I'm—"

"William, I know. Justin talks about you a lot. The guys practice at my house, so he's there all the time," Mary said, taking a sip from her cocktail.

"Well, I hope he hasn't said anything too bad," William said, leaving a chair between himself and Mary when he sat down.

"To tell the truth, I thought you were a metalhead like him, the way he describes you. 'He's fuckin' metal, man,'" she said, imitating Justin's dopey voice. "You know, that's the highest compliment one of these guys can give you—to call you 'metal' when your hair's not long and there aren't any more holes in your face than God gave you. Or should I say 'Lord Satan?'"

William laughed and took a drink of beer to try and hide his cheeks, which he knew had to be burning bright red. "What can I say, I guess he likes me."

"So tell me about your connection thing Justin always talks about," Mary said.

William buried his face in his hands. "I can't believe he told you that. I mean, it's just something I was thinking about and brought up to pass time." He wanted to scream.

"No, from what he tells me about your conversations, it's really interesting. I mean—" Mary began, but a distorted power chord rang out, and Justin shouted into the mic: "We are Angelfuck!"

The band began to play and Mary rolled her eyes in frustration. She scooted into the chair that separated them and leaned in close to William, her face in the curve of his neck and shoulder, her mouth inches from his ear. "It's just that I teach kindergarten, and between that and these guys debating over who's better, Maiden or Priest, I never have interesting conversations. So tell me about your theory."

William told her about human connectedness and all of our toiling as being attempts at connecting to the world at large. They talked and debated and he tried not to sound too passionate or crazy. She told him about her school and her brother and who knew what else, because William was focusing on the feel of her breath on the hairs he didn't know he had on his ear and neck. Angelfuck played fast, loud, and hard while Justin screamed to the high-hung rafters, and a fight broke out in the back of the bar, but William couldn't take his eyes off Mary, who he hadn't noticed was so beautiful when he first saw her.

"Thank you, Redrum! Hellfire and Grindstone is next!" Justin shouted, then threw the mic down on the stage and jumped off and walked to the table. "How were we?" he said, still shouting. He was covered in sweat and jumping up and down.

William broke his concentration on Mary and looked up at Justin. "Great, man. You guys were great. It was metal."

"Thanks, bro. I need to go help clear our stuff off the stage. I'll be back and we're gonna get ripped."

William turned his attention to Mary. "You ready to get ripped?" he asked, mock jumping up and down.

"If only," she said getting up. "I have to get up early to tutor some of the older kids at my school. But you could walk me to my car."

She was parked a few blocks up the street. A cool wind had blown in from up north, making the air smell sweet over the stink of downtown on Friday night. It blew hard and was refreshing after the packed bar. Mary leaned into William and he put his arm around her, drunk from more than the beer he'd had.

"I had a good night, William," Mary said when they got to her car.

"Me too," he said through his smile.

"I'd like to see you again," she said. She wrote her number down on a sheet of paper and handed it to William. "I know you're unemployed, so maybe you can come over and I'll cook for you."

"I'd love that," William said, folding the paper gently and putting it in his pocket.

"Well, call me," Mary said and leaned in for a hug. William squeezed hard when he hugged her, and she gave a laugh. When she pulled away from him, she gave him the slightest of pecks on his cheek. "Bye."

He stood and waved as she drove off. Walking back to the bar, William saw in his reflection in a storefront window that there was a lip print on his cheek, and he thanked the whale whose blubber, William imagined, painted Mary's lips and marked William to remind him that she had, in fact, existed.

In the shadow of the worst day of his life, William was reluctant to feel happy. Good things never happened to him, much less in such dark times. He was left thinking of all of the things that could go wrong. Could she have not liked him? Was she only being nice? William knew his worries were unfounded, but worse had been known to happen to him. He stopped to wipe his cheek before going back into the bar. In doing so, he was saying goodbye to the external proof, but within him remained something alive and so close to real happiness that it scared him—there to remind him of his brief, beautiful connection to Mary.

He felt the void again, but it fought with the area on William's face that had been given a piece of Mary. He tried to convince himself that it was all going to work with her, the future he could almost make out on the horizon. He tried to compose himself so that he wouldn't be a downer for Justin and his band. He walked into the bar knowing that there was a real chance with Mary. A chance to get close to someone, to love them, to not be alone. And if it didn't work out, William still had a job interview on Monday at City Bakery.